Meeting Yama

MANOJ V JAIN

notionpress
.com

INDIA · SINGAPORE · MALAYSIA

Notion Press

No.8, 3rd Cross Street,
CIT Colony, Mylapore,
Chennai, Tamil Nadu – 600004

First Published by Notion Press 2020
Copyright © Manoj V Jain 2020
All Rights Reserved.

ISBN 978-1-63633-548-3

Other books by the same author:

- *The BNO, Sex, Life and Hookah*
- *The THC, Under a Gibbous Moon*
- *Balraj*
- *Ramona*
- *Dystopia*
- *A Man from Mandu*

This book is dedicated to

the **Big 8**,

BMPTR

D2 Basement and

M2VFS2

Maybe we were meant to meet, maybe we had met before, maybe we will meet again…whatever it is, it has been fun traveling together on this journey of a lifetime.

"What you seek, is seeking you."

–Rumi

CONTENTS

AUTHOR'S NOTE

Before I proceed with the author's note, there are three people because of whom this book exists. This book had been abandoned three times, but I persisted thanks to Shelina, Nandina and Jasma, who read the chapters as I wrote them and answered my innumerable questions and assuaged my doubts. They encouraged me to complete the book over several months and I am truly grateful for the hand-holding, which I needed at that time.

Meeting Yama was not an easy book to write and I have had to draw a lot from my energies to put it in word. The concept had been in the back of my mind for a while but a lot of different experiences have led me to pen this book: an epiphany in Varanasi, an exposure to various teachings and practices as well as a series of dreams.

I have always found it difficult to read non-fiction, especially about spirituality and philosophy. However, if the same concept is narrated through a parable or a story, then it engages me. Mythology has always been fascinating to me but I have normally stayed away from it in my writings, but in this book, I have included a lot of stories that many may have heard as kids very often to get across a point.

I am also very thankful to Annie, my yoga teacher, and to Neema, who has taught me so much.

Meeting Yama is a journey that we all undertake.

As I have said on the back cover, if the book has reached you, then there is probably something you will learn from it. I am happy to have written this book.

Manoj

September 05, 2020

Chapter 1

How Amrit Came to Varanasi

*"It takes only one voice, at the right pitch,
to start an avalanche."*

–Dianna Hardy

"There is a voice that does not use words. Listen."

–Rumi

Amrit boarded the aircraft from the rear doorway. A young air hostess greeted him courteously and he smiled absentmindedly. He found his seat and put his little bag in the overhead storage. He sat comfortably, his thin frame fitting in the narrow window seat and he stared out of the little oval window. He felt his cell phone vibrate and saw two messages. One was from his cousin, Bharat, and he decided to ignore the message. The second message was from Gagan. *Hope you are doing well. I'm missing you. The bed already seems empty. Be well and message me when you land.* Amrit read it and smiled; he wished Gagan could have traveled with him. Quickly, he typed back, *I am fine. It's lonely without you – I wish you could be with me. But you know I had to make this journey as a final act. I will message you. Take care – I have left some hummus for you in the fridge. Love you.*

The announcements soon started and he paid rapt attention to all the safety instructions. Somehow, he always imagined that he would experience an emergency landing where he would need to use the life jacket and the rafts that would spring out from the doors. He always went through the printed safety card in each seat pocket too. His neighbor tapped him and asked, "How long is this flight to Varanasi?"

"It is about two hours' flying time," Amrit replied.

"Are you going for work or as a tourist?" he asked.

"As a tourist," said Amrit, but continued hastily, "I am taking my mother's ashes to submerge in the Ganga."

"Oh, I am sorry to hear about your mother's death," said the neighbor.

"Thank you, but my mother passed away a year ago. I had decided to put her ashes in the Ganga whenever I could. Finally, I have found the time and energy to make the trip."

They chatted a little and then, slowly the food service started. After eating the preset meal, Amrit closed his eyes, trying to sleep. *Why am I going to Varanasi?* he thought to himself. His mother had never mentioned it to him ever in her life; this was something he wanted to do based on a whisper he had heard or imagined he had heard. He looked at his phone, out of habit, and opened Bharat's message. *Hope you are okay Buddy. You have really been a good son. Have a good trip to Varanasi. Call me when you are back in Mumbai.* Amrit looked out of the window at the clouds below them and started reminiscing.

It all started a little over two years ago when Bharat, my cousin, called me up.

"I have a friend who needs some help with digital marketing," he said

"What kind of help?" I asked

"A friend of mine has started a small business of her own and wants to reach out to the locality to publicize it. I told her that you will be the best person for the job."

"What kind of business has she started?" I asked.

"She communicates with animals telepathically," he replied. "You know, if your two pets don't get along and you need to understand what's going on in their mind and things like that."

I whistled. "I've never heard of people communicating telepathically, least of all with animals," I said. "Is this friend all there? She sounds a bit cuckoo to me."

"She's alright," he said. "I've known her since school. She was crazy about animals even then. I never really believed in what she did, but now, I do somewhat believe in her telepathic communication. A few months back, another school friend of ours' dog went missing and she communicated with the lost animal and told the friend where he could find his pet."

"Tell your friend to call me later in the week. I have to do some research on this before I can market it for her. Or maybe you don't have to tell her and she will know that telepathically," I said, cracking a sad joke.

"Well, she needs to see a photo of the animal to communicate with it. I will send her a good one of yours," he retorted back. "Basically, she's started a business of her own and needed some social media publicity. I said you would help at a low cost."

"Hmm," I said, "I will be charging something. I cannot do it for free, you know, unless she is really someone special to you."

"Nah," he said, "charge her a minimal amount but keep it in mind that it's not a big business. She can't pay much."

"What did you say her name was?"

"It's Penaz. And it is not what you're thinking of, you ass!"

After the phone call, I got busy with my other work and forgot about Penaz and her telepathic communication with animals. That evening, I went out for a long walk and then to the pharmacy to buy my mum's medicines.

At night, I lay in bed, working on my computer. Once I completed the scheduled work, I remembered that I had to do some research on non-verbal communication with animals. Initially, I sniggered, derisively, to myself at the thought of telepathically talking to pets but then I decided to keep an open mind and set aside my preconceived notions since it was my client's line of work. I started my search on the internet and I was surprised at how popular the topic was. I opened a few sites that the search engines threw up and started reading so I would be prepared if and when Penaz called me. There were all kinds of posts on the net, some were downright offensive, where the writer said that a person simply could not communicate with animals, and if you wanted to communicate with a dog, then you would need to smell butts, learn to bark and pee on hydrants. On the other hand, there were many other sites and posts where there were people who gave glowing testimonials. I kept scrolling and reading, finally reaching the conclusion that it boiled down to faith and belief. I decided to hear what the client wanted from me and her budget and would then continue on from the preliminary readings that I had just done.

I shut my laptop and tucked myself in, browsing the messages on my phone as it charged by my bedside, too tired to get onto the Grindr app that I usually mused over before I slept.

I awoke early the next morning as there was a lot of work to be done. Of late, I had been feeling that I was not spending enough time with Aai. While Ranjana got mother out of bed and cleaned her, changed her adult diaper and gave her a sponge, I got busy preparing the morning tea and biscuits for the three of us at home. I tried to contribute more in the little household tasks as Aai got more dependent and less capable of doing any work.

Since I was working from home, I had told myself to maintain discipline and a tight schedule. I would finish my bath and change into semi-formal clothes. My office was part of the living room; I had set up my desk with the laptop and printer; the shelves and drawers had all that I needed for work. The adjoining table was full of notepads and pens and often worked as a spare table when I called my freelance creative or copywriter in. Although business was good and I had a lot of work through word of mouth and repeat clients, I tried to keep my expenses low. Maybe that was to do with my childhood and upbringing. When my Baba left us, it had been a difficult period for us. I was eight years old. I remember the day clearly. Aai and Baba had had another huge fight. They thought or rather preferred to assume that I was sleeping in my room and would not hear it but I, however, would stand at the door, my ear pressed against it, to try and listen to them. The themes of the fights would vary but it ended in the same way with Baba sleeping on the couch in the hall or walking off. Sometimes there were words like alcohol that I understood but there were many that I didn't. Over time, I began to dread it when my father would remove the alcohol bottles from his cupboard and get ice and lemon from the kitchen because I knew those were the signs that there may be another brawl coming; these were symbols like a weather vane rotating above a house at a horrible speed, indicating the brewing of a storm. The sight of soda bottles with ice and lemon next to them would forever make me a tad uncomfortable even in later adult years. Aai would come to tuck me in bed on those days and as she lay beside me, often asking about school, we formed a strong bond. I began to think of my father as evil and it had been more than once that I imagined myself in some schoolboy fantasy of having a duel with him to save the damsel, my mother, in distress. The night that he left us for good, the fight was louder and longer than ever; I heard a glass bottle break, a metal clang. I heard a thud, I heard a scream; I hid under the blankets and closed my eyes tight, putting my hands over my ears and saying prayers to an invisible God to help. The next morning when I awoke, Baba was nowhere to be seen although the room yet had his presence hanging in it, like the smell of stale wet mop cloth lingering even after you have disposed of it away. Aai was attempting to put on an air of composure and I just went and hugged her. I loved the smell of the thrifty soap that emanated from her and her starch-crisp cotton sarees; they gave me a sense of comfort. Years later, sitting in a psychiatrist's chair, I mentioned this smell as a memory that would give me security and peace and I latched on to it for therapy. She did not say anything to me that morning but I saw her hair was not in place, which was unusual for her at any time of the day, and there was a bandage on her arm. She had an air of not being there at the moment, a vagueness as she carried out her daily chores to send me to school. I was surprised that she had not gotten ready for her office and seemed to have missed her morning prayers too, and she forgot to remind me to take blessings from the deities in our little temple at home before I left for school.

The temple was a small wooden box with two shelves filled with many Hindu gods and also a couple of saints that my parents believed in. My mother had great faith in Sai Baba so his picture was prominent. Multicolored lights blinked on top, there was a plastic hibiscus at the feet of the gods, besides the essence sticks that we lit each morning. We lived in a small ground floor apartment in Matunga, in a colony of three-storied buildings. We, like the other people in the housing complex, had no notions of grandeur: we knew we were simple middle-class folk and we were proud of it. Ours was a modest flat, with two bedrooms, each with an attached toilet. We had all the trappings of our upbringing; our phone lay on top of a mini carpet made especially for it; we had a cover for our TV and we had cute stuffed toys on our mantel. We ate from steel plates and our cutlery, glasses and napkins were mismatched. A fourteen-day trip to Europe by a local tour operator with other like-minded families was the extent of our aspirations provided we were served hot Indian vegetarian meals. We saved on power bills, conscientiously turning off the lights and the fan even when we stepped out of the room for a minute, trying to use the electricity guzzling geyser to the minimum. Aai worked in a Government job, which gave job security and regular salary increments as per the pay scales. She dressed in her cotton starched sarees and took the bus from outside our house that took her straight to the office. My school was nearby and I would go walking along with the other children from our colony.

One day, after a parent-teacher meeting, she came home with some samosas and a tiny sponge cake. "What is the occasion?" I asked her.

"Your teachers all praised you," she said.

I knew that was not true, for I was not a bright student in class and never shone, happy to be inconspicuous and middling but I did not say anything to her. The smell of the samosas made me forget everything and the delight of having a cake for no reason that night for dinner made me happy. After dinner, Ranjana and Aai cleaned up the plates and she changed into her nightgown. She came to my room and spoke in general about studies and school. Then, softly, she said, "Amrit, why did you not tell me that the other children in school tease you?"

Her voice was gentle but her words hurt me and dug into my skin. It was one thing being teased in school but much worse when your family knows about it. It was like a veneer of self-respect being snatched away, rendering one naked in front of one's family. "They don't tease me, Aai," I said, a quiver coming into my voice, my face shrinking and giving my lie away. Aai never said anything but just hugged me; much against my wishes, water welled in my eyes and spilled out.

"Why did you give me such a horrid name?" I said sobbing, "The other children call me Amrita as if I am a girl."

"Amrit is the nectar of the gods," she said gently, hugging me yet. "You were God's gift to us; the nectar sent for Baba and me, so we called you Amrit. You were been born after many years of our marriage when we had given up all hope of having a child. God heard our prayers and said he is sending us someone special and that is why it had taken so long."

Gently, she continued, "Let them call you whatever names they want. Remember this, that you are my nectar, my Amrit. You are special." And we left it at that.

Occasionally, when Aai thought I was asleep, I could hear her speak on the phone. From the tautness of her voice, the talk of money, the sarcasm and the bitterness in the words, I knew she was talking to Baba. I was both angry and relieved that he never contacted me or asked for me and I never spoke to him again. I did ask Aai about him and his whereabouts when I was a few years older but I never got a reply that soothed me or satisfied me. I did have him visit me in my dreams a few times and with every passing day, he grew bigger in my mind, larger than life, more male than other men, a drinking, womanizing man. During my teens, I was appalled when he featured in an erotic dream and I felt guilty when I realized that maybe I was attracted to him sexually. I quickly banished that unholy thought from my mind and I sat in front of the gods in our home temple that day and prayed, asking for help and purification.

I was in college by now but my lithe, petite body was yet that of a schoolboy. Those days we had such few choices in subjects. I was definitely not studious enough to pursue science and I had no inclination toward business, so I had chosen the study of arts, which in those days, was primarily a stream of education for girls. Among many other concerns, it was my sexuality that was the primary cause of worry to me: I was coming to terms that I was more interested in men, rather than women, and I did not know how to handle it. I would travel to college by bus and find myself attracted to the tougher, older men, especially those in uniform or with a stubble; I would try and sidle up near them so there would be body contact. I was always worried that someone from my colony or college would see me and my heart beat faster than ever; I would be worried that I would be branded and teased once again. I knew I was effeminate in my body and my gait but I would try and imitate the mannerisms of the other boys, would try and deepen my voice as I answered the phone and attempt to be just another regular man. On other evenings, I would spend my evenings hanging around the urinals at Shivaji Park or walking on the semi-secluded beaches close to my house. I knew Aai would find out sooner or later and was at a loss of how to mention this 'problem' to my mother but, I did not have to worry too long on it: Aai had figured out my 'affliction' as I thought of it then and gave me broad hints that she knew. I felt bad for her, as I was aware that this would not bode well with our middle-class mentality in which we always strived to be normal, but she took it in her stride and (I suppose) blamed it on Baba. Actually, I now realize in hindsight, that most people already know before one actually comes out of the proverbial closet; it is so much easier being open about it; it is just stressful keeping it a secret. One day, over dinner, she caught the bull by its horns and openly discussed it with me. I was tight-lipped at first and even feebly attempted denial, but soon the flood gates opened and I 'confessed'. She explained that there was no reason to feel guilty and it was fine but to be careful of the world. Homosexuality was not a comfortable word in our socio-economic class, in our neighborhood or in our country itself plus there was this new-fangled disease that seemed to target the gay community. That night I slept a lot easier. Aai and I never discussed this topic again, although she had caught me a couple of times, years later in different embarrassing situations, like finding my gay porn or me wearing her glass bangles when I did not expect her and Ranjana to be home early.

Ranjana was our live-in help since as far back as I could remember. She had come as a young woman in trouble. My mother's sister had contacted us and asked if we could help this lady from the village. She was a young widow and needed to leave the village as she was being harassed. My mother's sister was a grass-root social worker and we were used to requests like this from her. She often recounted stories of the poor conditions of the people she would encounter and how she tried to rehabilitate them. When Ranjana came, she was a thin waif-like creature; we did not know her exact age because she had no proper documents but we figured she would be in her mid-twenties, a good ten years older than I was at that time. My mother treated her as a companion, both single women now, although Ranjana was more than twenty years younger than her. Ours was a simple, no-fuss household and over time, Ranjana managed it efficiently and dedicatedly. As years passed, she became part of the family although she never crossed that final barrier between the house owner and the help. Over time, she had understood my preferences for men, either by herself or in discussion with my mother, but she accepted it and I am glad that she was as respectful and loving and caring toward me as she had always been.

Once Aai reached retirement age, she had to stop working; she and Ranjana would sometimes get into arguments, as Ranjana was used to running the house in her style and timings and without interference. But the two slowly found a balance and peace was maintained. I was in my mid-twenties by then and had entered the job market. I had joined an advertising firm that accepted differences, rather it welcomed them and none of us working there were uncomfortable or judged strongly. It was there that I learned many things, to accept myself and others in the same way that my colleagues let me be free to toy with my own style; I would sometimes sport long hair, or pierce my ears or keep a man bun, wear Ganesh kurtas or neon geometrical printed bandanas. While it does not seem so revolutionary now, it was fifteen years ago when I was twenty-five. Young people do not realize how lucky they are to be born in today's times when everything is more easily acceptable than it was when I was young. It was in these offices of advertising firms, open-minded and accepting, that I experimented with things that my middle-class morality had always stopped me from trying. I let go of my inhibitions and became less judgmental in the process. Computers, coding, dot coms were all buzz words and I took to the emerging technologies, putting in hours at work, mastering them. Therefore, naturally, it was I who was appointed to handle newer marketing platforms like Facebook, which had never existed before.

A few years passed and I was working harder than ever, heading a lot of new projects. I had odd office hours and I sometimes reached home early in the morning, having worked all night in the office or being with one of the many lovers that I had found. Those were promiscuous years but I was careful never to call any of them to my house. One evening, as I returned from work, Ranjana opened the door and told me that she needed to speak to me about Aai. I assumed that they must have had a bad day and Ranjana wanted to offload. But I was wrong for she had a worried look about her, not an exasperated one. "Something is not right with Aai," she said, "she seems to be forgetting some basic tasks like how to pin her saree." I kept quiet and Ranjana continued with a bit of puzzlement in her voice. "She also gave the milkman more money than needed." That took me by surprise. I knew that Aai was very particular about finances and I have never known her to part with an extra rupee in any circumstance.

I looked quizzically at Ranjana. "Let me speak to a couple of people I know," I said.

I had been a late child; Aai was nearly forty years old when I was born. She was in her mid-seventies by then. I called Leena, my friend, whose brother was a doctor and explained the situation to her. Based on his questions, and preliminary analysis, we went through many tests as recommended by him and met various specialized doctors; the final conclusion was that Aai had the onset of Alzheimer's. I started to read a lot about the disease and how rampant and degenerative it was and I knew that life for all of us was about to change. I sat with Ranjana and explained the situation to her; we decided to observe the changes closely.

At around that time, I got a phone call from an unknown number. A rather raspy voice informed me that my father had died and I was needed to light the funeral fire. I sat in my room, still and awash with many mixed feelings that I could not make sense of. I decided to breathe slowly and compose myself. At the same time, I did not know what to tell Aai, especially in this condition. I discussed it with Ranjana and we thought it was only fair to tell mother that she was now a widow. I do not think that she and Baba had officially divorced ever. I went to her room and walked up to her armchair. She loved sitting on it and reading her magazines, carefully turning page by page. I knelt on the floor and put my hands on her knees and she looked at me and smiled. She placed her hand on mine and I was surprised to see how wizened it looked, shrunken and full of wrinkles. "Baba has passed away," I said. She did not respond and so I held her hands firmly in mine and repeated, a little louder, "Baba has passed away. He is no more."

I saw a flash of anger in her eyes and a touch of color flare up on her cheeks. In a garrulous voice, she said, "Tell him never to show his face to me. He can go and live with that whore of his."

"I am going to his funeral," I said resignedly. "He is dead," I explained in case she had not comprehended my first statement.

"Everyone goes. We all have to go," she said sounding philosophical, quite behaving like a scene she must have seen in a film. Ranjana was standing on the doorway and weeping, not for Baba but for Aai's condition.

I got up to leave when she said, "Baba is dead?"

"Yes," I said. She sighed deeply, tilted her head back so it rested at on the armchair and closed her eyes.

My father had a traditional cremation, not the electric ones that most people had shifted too. I had called Bharat to come as I was nervous to go alone and did not know how I would handle myself. I was glad he accompanied me, for I did not know anyone else there either. There were just five men and I followed the instructions of the priest and mechanically carried out the ceremony. Once the logs caught fire, we were told to sit in the enclosure, on the side until the flames engulfed the body entirely. The five other people sat with me for a while and then they got up to leave. I noticed they were old men too, looking rather shabby, maybe my father's friends or neighbors. I did not know how they had my mobile number nor did I think it was appropriate to ask.

Aai's decline was faster than what was the norm. One day, when I was at work, Ranjana called me up, panic in her voice. "Aai has left the house," she cried. I felt my feet turn to jelly; my mind began racing and my hands were trembling. "I am coming," I managed to splutter on the phone. I rushed out of the office and had just sat in the taxi when Ranjana called me once again and said that Aai was found wandering in the colony compound, quite unaware of where she was.

I did not return to the office that day but came home instead, anxious and very troubled. I sat with Aai and spoke to her gently and calmly but my mind was racing. Ranjana met me in the living room and explained that she had gone to wash the clothes; when she came out, she saw Aai was not in her room. We both realized that it was not possible to have a single caregiver for Aai. I had also been on an Alzheimer's caregiver forum and knew there was a lot that one could do to reduce the cognitive decline. It involved time and patience and it was definitely not Ranjana's cup of tea as she had the housework as well. The costs of the specialized Alzheimer's specialists who came home to play games with the patients were prohibitive for me and so was a full-time nurse. That night, I lay in bed and thought the matter thoroughly. I knew that my career was rising rapidly, especially since digital marketing was a high growth area for most companies. On the other hand, it was Aai who had given me as perfect a childhood as a parent could in those circumstances as well as accepted me and made me accept myself. I knew it was a no brainer. I would quit working outside and stay at home with her. I would be the caregiver; we needed no one else. I took the decision with happiness and joy. As my thoughts continued, I decided to convert one part of the living room into my office or study and start my own digital marketing firm from home.

At first, the company that I worked for suggested that I take a two-week break for medical reasons and use the time to work things out personally but I was sure that I wanted to be with my mother in her twilight years. Once they agreed to let me go, they used my services as a freelancer, giving me a decent amount of work. I made changes in the living room layout, bought relevant furniture, got hi-speed Wi-Fi and started my home office. Slowly, my work and income kept increasing as technology and online apps made it easier to work from home, to receive payments and to have virtual client meetings. If needed, I would go out for meetings or for coffee to meet a friend. As Aai grew frailer and more incapacitated, my personal life schedule changed too. I would wake up early to make tea for the three of us while Ranjana would change my mother's diapers and clean the bedding. I sat with her for morning tea and chatted with her. Her responses were becoming more childlike but I had expected it from my readings on the disease. I would start work in my office early in the morning while a yoga teacher would come in at the same time for Aai. It was important to keep her body active and Ranjana would take her for a walk around the colony twice a day. We had forgotten the yoga sir's name as we only referred to him as Masterji. He spoke chaste Hindi and he was from Rishikesh; he was respectful and soon he became part of our morning routine.

*****

Penaz called me the next day. She sounded full of energy and her voice was brimming with positive vibes. I could feel her gentleness over the phone as we spoke. She explained that she needed to publicize her telepathic capabilities to pet owners especially in the case of lost animals as well as for them to contact their pets that had passed away. She also ran classes for teaching this skill to people so she was looking for help from me to market these services online. She did not have any budget idea; she believed online publicity would be free. Although her business was not large enough to be a proper client, I entertained her since she was Bharat's friend. I was polite. I had no choice, for her manner of speaking was so kind that I could not be curt with her. I asked her to come to visit me at the home office the next day as the copywriter would be in too and we could discuss the project. I decided I could work pro-bono for this one and only charge her actual expenses.

Penaz came a little later than the appointed time. It was the start of the month and I was busy settling the salaries and paying the copywriter her fees as well. "I can sit and wait," she said in a soft voice.

"No, don't worry," I said, "let us finish the work."

The copywriter and I pulled our chairs facing her so it became more like a meeting. "Basically, I telepathically communicate with animals," she said. The copywriter, who was unaware of this new client, looked at me quizzically with a slight smirk on her face. Penaz ignored the look if she noticed it; she must have been used to it.

"How do you communicate with animals?" asked the copywriter, a tinge of sarcasm in her voice.

We were interrupted by Masterji, the yoga sir who wanted his monthly fees too. "I will wait on the side," he said, "you finish," and we continued our meeting.

"I believe that we are all part of one consciousness," said Penaz, a little tinkle in her voice, which was charming, since the subject was a strange one. "Since we are all a part of the same energy, one can communicate with other life forms, which are all extensions of the same energy." She noticed us looking blankly at her so she went on to explain, "Through the centuries, as we kept developing, we have lost many different senses; we seem to have forgotten the ability of non-verbal communication with other beings; over time, we seem to have lost our knowledge of the single consciousness."

Having worked for several years in the advertising industry, I was familiar with a lot of different concepts and offbeat thought processes. In my earlier days, early twenties maybe, I had experimented with a fair share myself, with different concepts like transcendental meditation, out of body experiences and alien abductions. I would smoke a joint once in a while but had relatively restricted my free-thinking spirit of late. Penaz sounded interesting and she believed in what she was saying but I was not convinced. My copywriter, on the other hand, had decided to challenge it and with an element of mirth, continued, "Just a small question – in what language do you communicate?"

Penaz did not look flustered; she seemed to have met many doubters and was familiar with the questioning patterns. "Consciousness does not need physical words. I think and mentally communicate with them in English. It's like an auto-translate."

I could see the exasperated look on the writer's face and I intervened. "It is certainly remarkable," I said to

Penaz, lest she would get offended. She was after all a client, even if a non-revenue generating one. "What would you like us to do for you? My cousin, Bharat, has said that you are a good friend and any friend of his is a friend of mine."

"Thanks," said Penaz, "Basically, I think I need a simple website made and maybe a Facebook page for this business. I am not business-minded at all and need to get some systems so that I can professionalize this."

I sighed to myself, internally, as this would be time-consuming and the project would be of a really small scale. "Do you have any budget in mind?" I asked.

"No," she replied.

"You don't have a budget," said the copywriter incredulously, "which means we can spend any amount?"

"I think she means that she has a zero budget when she says she has no budget," I said calmly.

Penaz smiled helplessly and I continued, "I will make a website. There may be a small expense to book the web address and buy some space on the cloud and I think we should definitely put a disclaimer along with all the services you provide. Could you also send me some testimonials from clients you have worked with?"

"The testimonials should be written," said the copywriter, with a sweet smile laced with black humor, "not telepathically conveyed."

"Sure," said Penaz, unfazed, "that sounds perfect."

"Let me email you all we need from you. I will also send you a format to fill and costs that you will have to pay. We will not add any of our charges," I said, ignoring the flashing eyes of the copywriter, "but you will have to bear actuals."

She smiled and said, "Thank you," and I felt something good stir within me. I stood up and led her to the door. Just before she left, she added, "I once did a session of telepathic communication with an autistic child. Should I ask them for a testimonial too?"

"Yes," I said, "that will increase the scope of clients for you."

"Oh, good!" she said, "Then, I will send you a list of potential clients like patients with cerebral palsy as well as people who have hearing and speech impairments, mentally challenged people and patients who suffer from Alzheimer's disease."

My ears pricked up at the last word and I held her arm. "You mean you can communicate with all sorts of patients?"

"Yes," she said, "As I explained earlier, the basic fundamental is the belief that we all share one consciousness."

"I will wait for your email," I said a little eagerly, letting her go. Her words had put my mind into a tizzy, and many thoughts rushed in from all directions.

I was interrupted by Masterji, who, I had completely forgotten, was waiting for his monthly fees.

I returned to the task of paying the salaries. "Sorry, Masterji," I said, "to keep you waiting."

Masterji smiled and said, "Who was that lady?"

"A new client," I said.

"She is special," he said quietly.

I glanced at the copywriter and I was relieved to see she was busy on her laptop with headphones. I softly asked, "Special in what way?"

"She spoke about one consciousness, one awareness. That is the basis of the philosophy of the Upanishads and Vedanta."

"Do you think it is possible to speak non-verbally with other living things?" I asked.

Masterji smiled and said, "It is a matter of belief, I suppose. In olden days, it was common for yogis to levitate because they became lighter than air; they could live much longer, hold their breath for hours underwater."

"I think of all that as mythology," I said, my voice faltering.

"It has everything to do with breathing and meditating," said Masterji.

"So, you mean anyone can do it? I don't think this client who just went (referring to Penaz) has done years of breathing techniques or meditation."

Masterji smiled benignly, making me feel a bit foolish although I had no cause to feel like that. "You do not know what your client does or does not do. In any case, it depends on the person. Some people are more advanced in their birth path and already come with many gifts inside them while there are others who can develop these special skills here, in this lifetime."

I paid Masterji and went back to work but his words kept playing at the back of my mind. I was silent during lunch and Ranjana had to ask me twice if I wanted more *rotis*. "Are you feeling okay?" she asked

"Yes, I am fine," I said but I was still pre-occupied with the conversation with Penaz and Masterji. Out-of-context, I said to Ranjana, "I am planning to start yoga classes myself."

"That will be very good for you," she said, "It will help calm your mind. You work hard and take on too many responsibilities; yoga will benefit you."

And thus, each morning, began my classes with Masterji. He started coming in an hour earlier for my class, so he could continue with Aai's class after mine. We started with simple asanas and stretches along with breathing but I would get impatient as I wanted to jumpstart the process.

Masterji would calm me down, explaining that I had to keep building to more advanced yoga practices and we would have to start at the beginning.

"But it could take years," I said, worried that it would be too late, for my end goal was non-verbal communication with Aai.

"I cannot help you with that," he said, unwilling to allow himself to be pressurized by me. "There is no fixed time frame," he continued, "some students move faster and others slower. There are no rules for this."

"Please talk to me about the single consciousness," I would say to him, "teach me the meditation techniques and breathings to tap into the energy."

"This is not a switch that you can just turn on and off," Masterji explained patiently. We started our classes slowly, practicing alternate nostril breathing and then same side breathing; our attempt was to align the flow of life-giving breath, to open the different channels of warming energy of the sun through the right nostril and the cooling energies of the moon from the left. I began getting acquainted with different *pranayamas* and the logic of chanting the universal, primordial sound of *Aum* and its vibrations on the spinal cord, throat and brain, the benefits of humming like a bee and finally the timed inhalations, retentions, exhalations and retentions. This went on for a few months after which Masterji added the mudras. He smiled when I referred to it as yoga for the fingers and explained how each specific energy centers in the hands could play a role in bringing about change.

Aai's condition kept deteriorating; each evening, I would sit with her after work and try and play specifically selected special games on the tablet. She was physically mobile but she had started to speak lesser and lesser. The specialist who had tested her had said she had forgotten the concept of dates and days of the week, seasons and how to read the time. She may forget speech as well, he said, and finally, stop recognizing the household members. We wanted to slow that process as much as possible so Ranjana and I dug out the old photo albums and I would sit with black and white photographs (careful to hide the ones that had pictures of Baba) to help her jog her memory. She did not speak much, but she would stare at the images while I spoke to her at length about each photograph. We changed our diet to a vegetarian diet as my studies showed that meat was harmful to Aai's disease; Ranjana began assisting her to eat as well and we upped her medicine dosages. After speaking with my neighbor who would help us often, we employed a part-time maid who would come in every morning to help us now that Ranjana had become the primary caregiver to Aai.

Masterji then introduced me to the concept of meditation. At first, I would have to sit and close my eyes and concentrate on my breathing, feeling the coolness of the air in my inner nostril as I inhaled and the warm air on my upper lip as I exhaled. I had to keep count, but I found my mind wandering quickly, much as I would plan to concentrate.

"Do not worry," Masterji would say, "It takes time and practice." He went on to teach me different methods of meditating, some involved listening to sounds and others by being a witness to one's thoughts as a bystander. The one I liked the most was shutting my ears with a pair of earplugs to cancel the noise outside, close my eyes and concentrate on the sounds within. I strived to hear the beating of my heart, thinking at first that that would be the only sound I would hear but I never heard it; instead, I would hear the rhythmic, gentle sound of my breathing, like the sounds of a gentle ocean, and that would lull me to a different level of consciousness. I was so caught up in these new practices that I would often practice them at the end of the day too when I was alone in my room. I began to read more on these subjects in my free time and finally I asked Masterji to start the chakra meditation.

Masterji was happy to explain the three primary channels of primordial life energy and the position of the seven chakras where all three channels converged making them strong energy points. I realized this was what I was seeking and all the earlier exercises were preparing me for this knowledge. Under Masterji's guidance, I started to concentrate on these points, visualize the different imagery associated with them and chant the relevant sounds to harmonize and activate my energy flows. I could feel the synthesizing of my inner body-external body and the linkages of the basic elements of earth, air, water, fire and ether from the chakras to the fingers.

One day, Masterji asked me for a small terracotta *diya*, ghee and a cotton wick. I looked blank but asked Ranjana who said she would arrange it for the next day. He also mentioned a *chatai*, a straw mat which we had at home

"What is this for?" I asked Masterji.

"I will explain in detail tomorrow," he said, "once we have all the items with us."

The next day, Masterji requested me to draw the curtains shut so the room was unilluminated and shadowy; he asked me to sit on the straw mat on the floor

He pulled a chair in front of me and placed the little earthen lamp on it. He said that it was a special kind of meditation that will take me deep within myself, to touch the energy channels. When he lit the wick, the room was filled with the specific aroma of clarified butter in a terracotta lamp. It felt primeval with the natural elements, including the straw I was sitting on. It also had a spooky ambiance with a lamp burning in a darkened room mid-morning. "I hope this has nothing to do with calling spirits," I said cautiously.

"Oh no, don't worry," he said, "I am not into that kind of stuff. This is the meditative practice of *tratak*. I will teach it to you today and we can practice it over the next couple of days. Then, you can do it by yourself for it is to be done before sunrise for the best results."

I closed my eyes and normalized my breathing and on Masterji's instructions, I opened them and stared at the flame that was on eye level, about twelve inches away.

"Stare at the top of the flame and over time, it will engulf you," he said, "but for now, let your eyes water."

I was surprised that my eyes did begin to water within ten seconds of staring at the flame.

"Close your eyes now," he said as he blew off the fire, "and see the image of the flame in your third eye."

I could see it clearly in shades of royal blue, turquoise and green but orange in the center like burning coal, the shape of the third eye vertically. I sank into a deep trance as the image in my mind slowly faded, and in a distance, I heard Masterji asking me to open my eyes slowly. Place your hand on your heart and breathe deeply." Later he made me splash my eyes with water and then look at a tree or flowers.

I read up about tratak on the internet and decided to practice it daily, except on Sundays so that the outline of the flame would not get imprinted on my retina.

Over the months, I had completely forgotten the origin of the desire to learn breathing and meditation techniques; to tap the universal energy, to attempt telepathic communication that had started with my meeting with Penaz nearly a year ago. I had finished her requirements long ago but I realized that the pro-bono project had given me more than I could have asked for. My work continued to grow, I continued to meet friends at coffee shops and bars and I yet met lovers but now there was an internal power that had quelled my impetuousness. One afternoon, Leena, my friend, and I were hanging out in my living room. We were sprawled on the sofas, each talking and looking at our Instagram at the same time, the kind of chilling out where you can be who you want to be. I got a sudden feeling, it seemed totally out of the blue, that I could send Leena a message. I got up and went to my desk nearby and wrote the number '43' on a piece of paper and put it in an envelope. It was a number I had chosen completely randomly. I said to Leena, "Hey, listen for a moment. I need to do an experiment for a project that I am working on."

I sat facing Leena and stared into her eyes. I told her, "I will send you a number from 10 to 99. It can be any number; you have to try and guess what I am sending to you. I will first throw the first number; then, I will send the second number and finally both of them as a two-digit number." Leena nodded at me with a blank face, no idea of what was going on. We both closed our eyes and I began to picture a number – 4. It was thick, sometimes 3-D, sometimes studded and sometimes legibly handwritten. It took me just five seconds to keep visualizing the number '4' and mentally I shouted, *Leena, the first number is '4'*. I then began to concentrate on the next digit – 3. Again, I projected this to Leena who was clueless to what I was doing but was cooperating with me to receive the data. Finally, I thought of the number '43' and mentally threw it to Leena and began chanting in my mind, *Leena, it's '43'*. I seemed to get more vociferous (of course all that was in my mind itself); I was silent on the surface and I shouted one last time, *"Leena '43', it's '43'."*

The whole exercise lasted less than twenty seconds; Leena opened her eyes before me and dully asked, "Was it '43'?" I was euphoric. I was stunned. I was ecstatic. I knew Leena might be judgmental and find it strange so

I said, "No, the number I had thought of was '82'," and tried to look crestfallen.

"Bummer," she said and we continued hanging around on the sofa. "Amrit what kind of nutty experiment was that? You know there is no such thing as telepathy"

I smiled at her, pretending to be sheepish. "Hey, I had to try something for a concept I was thinking of for a client. I don't know what got over me," I said, "I guess it was a foolish idea."

That evening, I was super excited; I breathed myself into a calm state. I needed some more experiments before I knew for sure. I tried to send a message to Bharat to call me; I closed my eyes and pictured him and sent out a message saying, *Call Amrit*. I tried in the night, I tried in the morning again and then again later the next day but I received no message or phone call from Bharat. I decided to call him up, a bit disappointed that this experiment had failed, and we spoke in general about Aai's condition. I could not control myself, so I mentioned it casually, "I have been thinking of you these past two days."

"I am sorry, I have been too busy this past week at work. I will come to visit Mausi one of these days. I hope she recognizes me." I knew this experiment had failed but in mind, the success of the number '43' was too strong. I consoled myself by saying that maybe I needed to be physically close to the person and I decided I would start making my attempts in communicating mentally with Aai. She had reduced to saying no more than a couple of disjointed words and was not responding to most of what Ranjana or I were saying.

That night, I dwelled on what I wanted to tell Aai non-verbally. I also wanted to understand from myself the expectations that I had for a reply and whether I wanted any specific answer. As I thought about it, I realized that all I wanted was to tell her two things; firstly, that I love her and secondly, that she is no burden to me. Regarding responses, I wondered if I was even a receptor or how it would happen so I decided not to expect or look for any reply. I knew my intentions were clean and pure and no harm could come by sending this message to her. I decided to try this telepathic communication when I was close to her, preferably when I held her hands in mine or when I put my palms on her head.

Every day, I would sit with Aai for our morning tea together. At that time, I would hold her hands for a minute and send my message. I began adding this minute of quiet messaging during our evening tea time as well. It became a practice: Ranjana would get the tea for both of us along with Marie biscuits. I would dip the biscuit in the chai just like I knew she used to like it and feed her, and at the same time, I would send my two messages telepathically. I did not tell Ranjana about it; although I thought she would understand my intentions and even encourage me, it felt like something personal and sacred between Aai and me. Aai very often would take my hand to her cheek, or hold it tighter but was uncommunicative in words with me. Feedback is one of the most important tools of evaluation in digital marketing and checking for efficacy was second nature to me. Thus, I began adding one more line in my subtle messages to her. *Aai, if you are getting my messages, then please send me a sign.*

I knew I had to tell what I needed to be a credible sign, so I added, *If you hear me, then say the words 'Runtuntun' aloud to me.* I do not know why I chose such a random word; it was what came to my mind at the spur of the moment. I also needed her to physically say it because if it was communicated by her to me telepathically, then I would not know if I had imagined it.

Days passed and very often I would wait for her to say the magic word '*Runtuntun*'; although she would sometimes say unconnected words or attempt a sentence and then give up, the special feedback word was never mentioned. One day, several weeks later, I was sitting at my desk in the study working when I got the feeling that Aai needed me; I just knew that my mother wanted me to go to her. I rushed to Aai's room and she was semi-reclining on her bed, propped by two pillows behind her back and an acrylic throw covering her feet. Ranjana was in the room, dusting the furniture and she looked at me as I entered the room.

"All is well?" she asked me, seeing my face taut.

I wanted to tell her that I thought Aai had called me but I knew she would not understand. Instead, I went up to my mother and sat beside her. Instinctively, she bent her head toward me to rest it on my shoulders. I slipped an arm behind her shrunken, bony frame. I could feel her unsteady breathing on my shoulder and neck and I held her hand with my free arm. I kissed her forehead and I felt her face muscles relax and her lips twitched in an effort to smile. She opened her mouth and struggled, but she clearly said '*Runtuntun*' in a raspy voice and then slumped into my lap, her breath no more warming her body or mine. Tears welled in my eyes and I knew Aai had left me.

"Ranjana," I whispered. Ranjana looked up and saw the tears rolling down. Somehow, I was not upset with Aai's departure. Maybe it was because she acknowledged the messages that I had been sending her in the past few weeks, maybe because my meditation had made me calmer, maybe because I knew that she had died in my arms, maybe because I knew I preferred her to go before she lost more of her senses. It felt nice when the full colony came to pay their last respects to Aai but it was just a few of us who went to the electric crematorium. Bharat helped me with the arduous ceremony of sending off Aai on her final journey and I could not help but shed copious tears when we encircled the garlanded body for the last time, placing sandalwood sticks and pouring ghee on the shrouded figure. Finally, as I took the handle to slide the body in the electric oven that would consume my mother, my body started to shake and convulse. Bharat held me and helped me compose myself. "Be strong, Amrit," he said, "She is going to a better place."

I held the handle tightly, the doors opened and I could see the flames in the oven and feel the heat. I pushed Aai in the fire and at that time, I heard a voice in my head. "Varanasi," it said. It was so loud and clear that I knew it was not my imagination. It was not Aai's voice either; it was androgynous. I did not know who said it in my brain, but at that instance, I knew I would have to go to Varanasi. Maybe I would take Aai's ashes and submerge them in the holy waters of the Ganga; I knew Aai would have liked it.

The pilot announced that they would land soon and Amrit stopped daydreaming. He tightened his seat belt and his fear of flying and landing surfaced again. It would be good to be on the ground again and he waited for the touchdown. He was longing to reach Varanasi; he did not know what he was looking for but he knew the answer lay there.

CHAPTER 2

HOW SURYA CAME TO VARANASI

"They say if you dream a thing more than once,
it is sure to come true."

—*Sleeping Beauty*

"Trust in your dreams, for in them is hidden
the gate to eternity."

—Kahlil Gibran

Surya lay in bed unable to sleep at night. He changed his position, turning over to the other side; he saw the back of his wife. Her body was rising and falling, her breath heavy as was when she was in deep sleep. In a fortnight, they would be celebrating their twelfth wedding anniversary. He wondered for a moment whether he should reach out and caress her body under the sheet but decided against it. She would get disturbed and blame him the following day for her lack of sleep and the cause of the resulting foul day. He could picture her scowl as she did these days when she spoke to him and an involuntary shudder passed through him. He turned again, his back towards her again now and tried to go to sleep.

In the two weeks that passed by, Surya racked his brains wondering how to make their anniversary celebration special. Going out just the two of them, which he knew was what they should do, was out of the question as the dinner would be unpleasant for both of them. They would argue about the time, the choice of restaurant, the traffic on the way, what to order and whether the dish was edible. They would criticize the wine and assume that they had paid too much for too little. The evening would be anything but romantic; he had lived long enough with Damyanti to know the pattern they had fallen into. He knew it was futile to invite his family over, for Damyanti did not get along with them at all and she would either sit sullenly or might pass a rude comment. It did not seem fair to him to spend it with her parents either if spending it with his parents was taboo. He decided to suggest that they go out with friends who would be the buffer between the two of them; Damyanti and Surya would choose to sit as far from each other as possible in celebration of the day that they had come together in union as man and wife.

Lying in bed, he mused over how he and Damyanti had met. He had always felt it was fated because of the circumstances. He had been twenty-six years old then, living with his parents, working at his first job. They lived a simple life, with no excesses, but it was comfortable and happy; both his parents worked, both in the same job for many years as long as Surya could remember. They were not a very demonstrative family; there was no public display of emotion and neither did Surya witness angry outbursts between his parents nor did he experience being cuddled in bed. When he was young, his mother would stand at the doorway of his room, looking tired after a hard day's work after completing her chores, and wish him good night, as she turned off the light in his room. They lived within their means, sharing an old car between the three of them. His parents had taken holidays abroad two times in the past five years, both with a guided tour company, which served them Indian meals and hopped from one European city to another for fourteen days. Pictures of the holidays were on the side table in their house, his parents standing in front of the leaning tower of Pisa and another one of them with the Buckingham Palace in the background. A small souvenir, a mini metallic Eiffel Tower was perched between these frames, bought after a lot of bargaining on the streets of Paris. The group that they had traveled with was of similar age and profile and got along very well. The tour company would organize get-togethers once every six months to entice them to book for another holiday and the travelers would meet each other and reminisce about their holidays. On one such occasion, the group decided to bring their children for the get together as proposed by the company organizing it. There would be a stand-up comic who would perform for a short while, a slide show highlighting the new holiday packages for families and plenty to eat, drink and time to socialize. Surya's parents asked him to accompany them at that time, adding that it would be a lot of fun. They genuinely believed it and he was happy for them but he was reluctant to spend a weekend night with strangers, his parents' age. As the day approached, he agreed to drive them there and attend the presentation to humor his parents; he also knew that he had no other plans that evening so it was not a real sacrifice of something better. He carried a book along so that he could read when the presentation was going on.

At the event, he sat listlessly, trying not to look bored or disinterested. It was heartwarming to see his parents so excited and animated when they met the other fellow travelers and he was also a bit surprised to see this side of them. They introduced him initially but soon got so caught up meeting their friends that they forgot about him, which actually pleased Surya. He sat at one side, reading his book when someone tapped him from behind. He looked up with a startle and saw a girl, smiling at him. "Hey," she said, "do you remember me from college?"

He nodded, a bit in a daze and then smiled and got up from the chair. "Hi, Damayanti, of course, I remember you," he said, surprised that she would come up to greet him. It had been two years since they had left college and he was a bit flattered that she recognized him; when they were in college, he doubted she had known his name, even though they had passed each other in the hallways several times. "I am Surya," he said awkwardly, stretching his hand.

She smiled impishly, and said, "I am so glad you introduced yourself as I had forgotten your name. I saw you sitting here reading Kahlil Gibran and I came over to meet you for he is my favorite author."

Surya could have been crestfallen that it was Kahlil Gibran that drew a woman to him, and not himself, but instead, he felt elated that a girl like Damyanti had approached him.

Damyanti was there because her family was in the travel business and she was assisting her father, learning the ropes to take over. She had never been a traditional beauty, compensating the norms with her style, her attitude and personality. She dressed well, her trendy clothes that obviously came from the boutiques abroad and wore light makeup at all times. In college, Surya was too shy and awkward to have spoken to a girl like Damyanti and in all honesty, neither would she have socialized with him.

"Beauty is not in the face," she said quoting the poet Kahlil, as if reading his thoughts, "beauty is a light in the heart." It was a quote she had often used and knew it well.

Surya smiled at her, and answered back with a counter quote from the author, "You give but little when you give of your possessions. It is when you give of yourself that you truly give."

Damyanti's eyes opened a bit wide for a moment; she put her hand to her mouth and threw her head back a little and laughed. A beam of sunlight fell on her and at that moment, Surya knew he had fallen in love with her. "If I didn't know you better," she said, "I would think this is a pick-up line."

Seeing Surya looking flustered, she realized he was too simple to understand what she said, so she explained, "A guy asking a girl he knows from college to give of herself…ha-ha, it could be cheesy if I didn't already know the words from The Prophet."

"No, No I didn't mean that," he stammered, turning red.

Damyanti smiled and said, "Take my number and give me yours. They are starting the presentation and I need to go and sit with my Dad. I'll call you tomorrow."

When Damyanti actually messaged him the next day, Surya was surprised, for he had thought that was just a polite way for a girl to end the conversation. As per the plan, she fetched him for a drive that Sunday evening; Surya decided not to be conscious or nervous about himself, and so wore a casual checked shirt and jeans. He did select the cologne that his parents had got him from their last trip and looked at himself in the mirror twice before he stepped out. He knew he was blessed with good looks; his body was not athletic but well proportioned. He combed his mustache, something he did only on special occasions, like when he was going on stage for a prize in college, and settled his thick hair on his head with his hands. He sat in front, next to her, as she drove, the music playing a gentle tune, the seat belt tight against his body, the air conditioner blowing cool air that made him forget the sultriness outside. She was a better conversationalist than he was and she spoke with ease, making him feel comfortable and soon he was relaxed, laughing and joking with her as well. She drove to the fort at Bandra Landsend and parked the car; he could not help admiring how confident her movements were as she locked the car and walked toward the lookout on the sea. "I love coming here," she said.

Surya had come there often before with his friends, who found it a perfect place to smoke and share a beer. "Let's climb up the fort," he suggested.

"I've never been up. I don't know if my shoes will take the climb."

"It's hardly a few meters up and it's an easy climb. The view is superb," he said, sounding like a college boy. She saw the sun against him, his thick hair turning brown in the light as his body formed a silhouette and smiled. "Ok, but you have to lead me." During the climb, he had to hold her hand to help her up several times, and there was no trace of awkwardness.

After the initial first date, they began messaging each other often. Although he told himself that he was not bothered about their social class difference, he never did invite her to his apartment, nor did he ever take the old family car and Damyanti seemed comfortable with that for she never questioned him about it. She was always the one fetching him from work or his house or they would meet at a point and go out; he insisted on picking up the bill, whatever the amount was, for he had been brought up with traditional values where the man paid the check. Besides, he was earning sufficiently enough for it not to bother him. He went over to her office once and was surprised at how large their operations were; she breezily introduced him to her father and then guided him to her cabin.

That night, Damyanti took him to a new nightclub where she had been invited. They met up with a few of her friends and Surya was surprised to find that they were welcoming and friendly toward him; a small part of him did wonder if the elite circle of friends that she moved around with in college would accept an outsider and whether he would feel small or inadequate. But he knew that no one could make one feel little without their consent, and so held himself and his esteem up and enjoyed the evening. Damyanti stayed close to him and would put her hand over his arm once in a while. They both drank too much and as the evening progressed, Surya found his arm around Damyanti for the most part of the evening. They had sex that night. She was insatiable and a tigress, literally tearing his shirt and pulling out the belt that held up his pants because he was not unfastening it fast enough. She had one request: to keep the room completely dark, which Surya had no problem with.

She kissed him several times, her drunken breath fusing with his, her lipstick smearing over his face, his thick mustache grazing her tender skin. She fondled the hair on his chest with her nose, rubbing the thicker growth over the stomach. "I love a hairy man," she moaned. Her cell phone, lying on the table beside the bed vibrated with a message and in the blue light that emanated from the screen for a few seconds, he saw her cover herself self-consciously. He took the phone and pressed any button so the light came on again and put it close to her body. "Don't worry," he said, kissing her, "for beauty is the light in the heart," repeating the line from the quote that she had said when they first got acquainted. She smiled and opened her arms and he saw that there was a large scar, where the flesh had got burned, running from the side of her left breast toward the midriff. "I got it years ago when some boiling water spilled on me," she said, her voice in a whisper.

Surya bent down and touched it. He then kissed along it as she held her breath. She exhaled finally and pulled his head up and kissed him deeper and with more passion than before.

Damyanti got pregnant that night and a few days later when she found this out, she met up with Surya and told him the news, matter-of-factly, not knowing what response to expect. Surya reeled with the knowledge; he had had sex only a few times in his life, twice actually before he met Damyanti. He held her hand and asked her what she wanted, but she remained silent. Surya was in a daze himself, not actually in the right frame of mind to do what he did next; he went on his knees and asked Damyanti to marry him.

They had a hasty wedding ceremony. It was a small affair, attended by just the parents, close family and a few friends. Pregnancy did not agree with the bride and during the ceremony, she had to excuse herself to use the toilet. Surya had wondered if his parents were surprised at his hasty decision on marrying Damyanti, without any consultation with them, but there was little discussion in his household. During the wedding, both Damyanti and Surya read the passage from Kahlil Gibran on marriage, for it was the poet who had brought them together. They looked at each other with love, certain that this marriage was destined. Damyanti's parents knew of their daughter's pregnancy and therefore happily agreed to the unsuitable union, embracing and accepting Surya wholeheartedly. After the wedding, the newly married couple moved into a small but stylish apartment that her father had bought for his only child.

They were insanely happy in the first few weeks. They could not travel by flight after the wedding for an exotic honeymoon as it was not advisable for Damyanti to fly in her first trimester. So, they drove down to Lonavala, nearby, where Damyanti had a holiday home and stayed there for a week.

They spent long hours in the bedroom, huddled up, spending time with each other, forgetting to dress or eat.

They both knew so little about their spouse that there were many discoveries to be made, catching up to do, stories to tell, relationships to explain. And there was the enjoyment and pleasures of their bodies; Surya would cup her breasts in his hairy hands and nuzzle the nipple with his nose, his thick mustache tickling and grazing the soft skin, and then he would lightly bite at the areola. When Damyanti would playfully chide him, he would retort, "Let me enjoy them, Damu, before our baby monopolizes them."

He would make it a point to kiss her burn marks; Damyanti would sigh in relief as she had always been worried if they would revulse her partner. He would kiss her over her belly, not yet grown and whisper to his unborn child, even though it could not hear. Damyanti would shut her eyes tight, a smile on her face, convinced that she was the luckiest woman in the world.

They decided to go on a real honeymoon later after the baby was born; Damyanti went to work to her father's office the very next day after her honeymoon, the travel business that she was being groomed to inherit and Surya went to his office, a box of sweetmeats for his boss and colleagues, whom he had not invited to the wedding.

*****

After the miscarriage, life changed. Surya was helpless as Damyanti slipped into a deep depression that she could not climb out of. They visited a therapist and Damyanti showed some signs of recovery but her eyes had lost their spark, and her lips, their mischievous smile. She stopped taking care of herself, her skin grew dull and her hair, lifeless. Her parents were very worried and asked her to move in with them for a few days and so Damyanti went to stay at their house for a week of pampering and recovery. Surya would visit her after work and they would sit together on the dining table. Damyanti tried to make conversation but he could not see her expression as she wore dark glasses at all times, even in the house. His in-laws left them alone for privacy and Surya hugged his wife and tried to kiss her at the nape but Damyanti remained stiff and unresponsive. He gently slid her sunglasses from her face and her puffy, red eyes revealed her sadness. He held her hands and together, they wept.

Surya's parents came over to meet Damyanti but she remained clinically polite with them and they soon left, feeling uncomfortable with the silences.

Damyanti returned home and the couple decided to pick up the threads from where they had left it but it was easier said than done. Damyanti grew more silent and Surya indifferent, they threw themselves into work, making polite conversations in the evening. But in bed, in the darkness, they spooned each other, they let down their masks and slept snuggling each other.

As the months sped, and October came closer, there was an unspoken dread falling upon them, a shroud of pallor descending on them. It was the month that their child would have been born; Damyanti and Surya both wanted to be away. They decided to go for a vacation that month, a tradition they followed every subsequent October.

After a year, one night, as he turned off the bedroom lights, Surya gently asked Damyanti whether they should plan another baby. At first, Damyanti did not reply, but then later said hoarsely, "I am not ready yet." She would never be ready eventually and the topic was not mentioned again by Surya after his fifth unsuccessful attempt to cajole his wife to have another child. Their lives fell into a routine; Tuesday evenings were fixed at Damyanti's parents' house; they would go there straight after work and dine over there. Surya's father-in-law would open a good bottle of whiskey and the two men would sit in the living room and nurse their drink and talk about politics, the economy and the state of the business. Surya was very respectful of the elderly gentleman, who in turn also held his son-in-law in high esteem and both of them grew to love each other. He never felt totally comfortable with his mother-in-law. He felt that she blamed him for the pregnancy, miscarriage and everything that had ruined her daughter's perfect life. On Fridays, Damyanti went out with her friends. It had been awkward at the start when Damyanti said she would be meeting her friends for he had assumed that he was invited too. Gingerly, steering her words through an uncomfortable situation, she explained that it was only the old gang meeting without spouses. Surya was surprised, for he felt he was being excluded but he chose to be ungrudging about it, rather than bitter. Over time, Friday nights got reserved for Damyanti to go out with her group of friends, by herself and Surya was left to his own devices. At first, he would meet up with a couple of his pals, but later this evening became reserved for Jaideep, his neighbor. Slowly, it became the evening he most looked forward to. Damyanti and Surya kept Saturday nights free for going out as a couple, for most of the invites were for that weekend night. Sunday afternoons were reserved for lunch at Surya's parents' house; initially, they both went but as time went by, Damyanti would invariably have some excuse, which Surya never questioned, so he would go alone, have a more or less silent lunch, and then take a nap in his old bedroom. Sometimes, when he stared at the walls of the familiar room, the paint peeling in places, he wondered if he had made the right choices and whether he would ever be happy again in his life.

The following year, the couple went through a horrible patch. It was as if their brief marriage ended its life along with their unborn child. They had both started to drink together at home, they would drink too much or too fast and often lose control of their minds and tongues. They had begun letting out their inner frustrations in such evenings. "Are you ashamed of me that you cannot take me out with your friends?" he would ask and then they would battle it out saying horrid things that they would regret the next morning. Sometimes it was her accusing him of eyeing other girls, "You look like a '70s porn star," she smirked, drunk, "with that mustache and hairy chest";

on other nights it was their class differences or the scar on her chest or his working-class parents. They would repent later, knowing how badly the words hurt each other; they refused to apologize, substituting make-up sex instead, which would be harder, rawer, more passionate and just bordering on the violent, both releasing their anger, their unfulfilled dreams, their frustrations through the act, which is called lovemaking.

One weekend, about four years into their marriage, they sat together sober. It was a winter evening and Surya took his wife for a drive in their new car. "Where are we going?" she asked.

"To Bandra Fort," he said.

"Why are we going there?"

"I need to talk to you."

"Can't we do it at home?" she asked. He felt his temper rise. *Why can she not just come instead of probing and protesting?* he thought. But he held his counsel; he took her arm and pulled her toward him and kissed her forehead. "Because I want to go on our first date," he whispered.

"Let me put on a new dress then," she said, smiling weakly.

They sat on the ledge of the lookout, choosing not to climb up the fort, their legs dangling over the sea, looking at the Bandra-Worli sea-link bridge in the distance. They sat for an hour discussing how their marriage had failed.

They skirted the issue of divorce and decided to try and make things work. They promised to live with each other, to try and make love grow, to be respectful. They held hands and she kissed their clasped fists. It was nearly five years into their marriage, and while it was a necessary and positive talk, it also verbalized the fact that their marriage was non-existent and they would have to make a fresh start. It resulted in the death of passion between them; they became civil with each other, they became friends but not husband and wife. Their lovemaking was much less frequent and bereft of the energy of the earlier years.

Around that time, Damyanti's father developed a heart condition and requested Surya to take over one part of the business. Surya unhappily, but with Damyanti's consent, left his job and joined the family business, partly because of his respect for his father-in-law. Life for Surya had become fairly monotonous, guided by a routine and joining a business seemed exciting too. It was then that he met Jaideep.

A family moved into the neighboring flat: a nuclear family, with a husband, who Surya reckoned was about ten years older than he was, a wife and two sons. The boys looked like their father, one must have been just out of college and the other would have been just a couple of years younger. The man and his wife rang the doorbell and Surya opened the door.

"Hi, I am Jaideep," said the man brightly, "and this is my wife, Samira. We have just moved into the neighboring flat."

Surya invited them in and called Damyanti out to meet them as well. Surya did not know whether to call him 'uncle' or address him by the first name so decided to not use his name in the conversation at all. The new neighbors sat for a few minutes and left.

"He seems like such a positive man," said Surya to Damyanti after the guests had departed.

Surya would often see his neighbor when they waited for the elevator or sometimes when he took an evening walk in the building complex. They had many common topics that they would discuss when they met, sometimes the stock market or the performance of cricket teams or the newly released cars. One Friday, when Damyanti was out with her friends, Surya invited Jaideep for a drink and slowly this became a weekly event. Jaideep would come over with his drink and they would sit on the sofa in the living room. Surya would pull out his bottle of whiskey and get the snacks that were prepared for the evening. They would have the TV playing sometimes, either a news channel or a TV talk show and they would sip their drinks often passing comments or judgments, never contradicting each other. They fell into the pattern with ease and comfort as men can and both men valued their Friday evenings together.

One day, when Surya was leaving for the office, he met Jaideep in the foyer, waiting for the elevator in between their apartments and they got talking about the upcoming cricket matches. The lift carriage arrived on their floor and the doors opened and Jaideep's elder son came out. He saw both of them but did not greet either Surya or his father. The boy turned to look at them as they entered the elevator, and said to Jaideep, "I hope you are not taking my car today as well. I need it." Surya was taken back by the tone of the boy; it sounded a bit rude. Jaideep put his hand out to keep the doors from closing and gently said, "My car is yet in the repairs so I am taking the second car." The boy's expression showed no understanding and he continued, "Can't you use an Uber instead?"

Jaideep removed his hands and let the lift doors close instead of arguing with his son.

"I did not know that your son had bought a car," said Surya to Jaideep, "Which model is it?"

"It's a Wagon R," said Jaideep, "I had bought it as the second car for the family."

As the men parted once they reached the car park, Surya could not help but wonder if he would have been a good Dad. *Maybe I am not a father because I would not have managed to be an understanding father,* he reasoned with himself. *I would not be able to bear the rudeness of the children today.*

That Friday, he mentioned it to Jaideep after their second drink. Jaideep laughed, his stomach bouncing, "No one chooses family. You have to be happy with the cards dealt to you."

"True," said Surya, "although there is a theory that a family travels in clusters over several lifetimes."

"Then maybe I was born in the wrong cluster," said Jaideep smiling, showing no signs of remorse. Surya looked up from his drink sharply to look at Jaideep, but the older man continued smiling.

"I don't believe in clusters and rebirth. I have this family. If my children are rude, then I have myself to blame."

"Yourself?" asked Surya puzzled.

"Yes, for the children are a reflection of my upbringing."

"Your wife and your upbringing. They have so many more exposures, their peers, the books they read, their friends, teachers. You cannot blame yourself."

Hesitatingly he continued, "I could not help but be upset when he asked you to take an Uber. Aren't you the only breadwinner and the others consumers?"

"In a family, it's not about who contributes and who consumes," said Jaideep, "and they will grow up."

Over time, from Jaideep, Surya learned many things; he realized that being a father was more complicated than just having a child but the most important thing he learned was the attitude of positivity. Surya was surprised how Jaideep would try and be positive so he came up with a few hypothetical situations and Jaideep managed to find the ray of hope or the silver lining for each circumstance.

He also had a friend whom he could speak with, a person who was not a common acquaintance with Damyanti, a gentleman who would not judge him, someone he could turn to for counsel.

"Let's call it a night," said Jaideep, "I guess I have drunk enough for the weekend."

"Let's have one last one," said Surya, "I too have drunk a lot but let's take a last small round."

Jaideep settled back into his seat and Surya prepared the drink

"But enough about me, what about you? How long have you been married?"

"It will be nine years soon," said Surya, rising to fill his glass.

Jaideep looked at him and asked a direct question, "Are you happy?"

Surya coughed, startled, he spilled a little of the soda he was pouring. "I guess I am happy," he said with a sigh that gave him away.

"You guess that you are happy? That's certainly not a good answer. This is not a guess. Surya, you are much younger than I am. I know a lot more about life than you do."

Surya sipped his drink, and looked at Jaideep, waiting for him to continue.

"You need to go away sometimes," he said, "Wander, travel… You are young, you are free, and you have resources. Don't waste this opportunity." Jaideep took a gulp and finished his drink. Taking great support from the chair handle, he rose and unsteadily walked to the door.

"Next Friday then," he said and left.

That night, Surya slept early and deeply. He did not hear when Damyanti returned home, changed her clothes and slipped into bed. That was the night he had the first of his dreams, the one that would come again three times over the next two years.

*****

Surya woke the next morning, later than normal and turned to see if Damyanti was already up. He sat up, stretched his hands up in the air, rubbed his eyes; the dream he had last night was bizarre. Was it the alcohol from last night; he had drunk a couple of pegs too much or was it Jaideep's troubling question that had touched a chord deeper than he had expected? Why had he said, "I guess, I am happy!" How corny was that? Couldn't he have just given Jaideep a strange look and said I AM HAPPY but he knew he would not be able to say that truthfully.

He looked around to tell Damyanti about his dream but realized that she would have gone for a workout to the gym, downstairs. He lay back in bed, deciding to skip his exercise that morning, absentmindedly playing with the hair on his belly and pondered; the dream he had

had last night seemed so real. He dreamed often, hazily remembering his dreams on certain days, but last night was different for it did not seem vague when he awoke, it felt very real.

"Come to me," the voice had said in the dream, "I am waiting for you." He had seen a black stone, definitely an idol but in the darkness, the image of the stone statue with a garland of orange flowers was unfamiliar to him. He continued twirling a strand of hair and focused, a pronounced wrinkle on his forehead, trying to recollect if it was a man's voice or a woman's, but he could not identify it. It was more like a whisper of no determinate gender. In fact, Surya wondered if he had even heard the sound or if it was a thought email that had been placed in his head. It was a sound, he reckoned to himself, for the voice had reiterated its statement, this time more forceful, like a command. I WILL BE WAITING FOR YOU.

Surya looked at the clock and realized that he needed to get up and move. While taking a bath, he stood under the rain shower, soaping his body, thinking once more of the black statue and the cryptic message – COME TO ME. The imagery of the dream and the message seemed to have got stuck to him, for his mind would keep getting him back to it. He joined Damyanti on the breakfast table; she was sitting reading the news on her iPad, chewing a toast absentmindedly. She looked up and said, "Try the *poha* today, it's excellent. Just the way you like it." Surya sat at the table and carefully chose his words. "Damyanti, I had a strange dream last night," he started. She looked away from her iPad and looked toward him expectantly, "I dreamed of a black God and I got the feeling that I should visit a temple."

Damyanti looked at him and said flatly, "Tell Tushar at the office and he can book you to go to Balaji temple. He will make all the arrangements in Tirupati so you have a good darshan."

Surya knew that Damyanti had a lot of faith in Balaji for her parents were big devotees at his temple in Tirupati. His father-in-law had often hinted that Surya and Damyanti should go and perform a puja there and ask the Lord for a child but Surya knew it would take less of the Lord's blessing and more of his wife's acquiescence to having a child. He was disappointed that his wife had taken his dream so matter-of-factly while it had so much importance for him for it ran in the background of his thoughts.

Damyanti then added, "While you were dreaming of black gods, I was dreaming of business growth."

She sounded excited about what she was going to say, so Surya pushed back his thoughts of the dream and heard her. "People are looking for travel experience; they no longer want the regular stuff that the earlier generations wanted. They need tailor-made packages. I was thinking we should develop this side of the business. We can select some destinations that are less known and build unusual travel experiences around them."

"Yes," said Surya, "it sounds exciting. If you want, I can pursue it with a couple of the guys from the office. Let's work on the idea and come up with something. We can tie-up with a boutique hotel in that area or Airbnb properties for that market segment."

"Great," said Damyanti, "Get Beej *bhai* with you on the team. He's traveled by road within India and will have quite a few insights."

As he mulled over it, Surya realized that Damyanti was right: his dream of a beckoning idol seemed like fantasy and even childish especially when compared to the concrete business development dream projects of the real world. A sliver of thought entered his mind that maybe he should discuss his dream with Jaideep but he realized how foolish it may sound to others and decided against it.

With the initiation of the new project, Surya began to travel within India a lot more than before. As Damyanti had correctly surmised, Beej was an asset for this project and together the team had identified a few locations. Surya would visit the place, sometimes accompanied by Beej, on other occasions he would travel by himself. Damyanti accompanied him when he visited Bikaner; they stayed in a fabulous old haveli and sampled the local foods, making voice notes for their team to follow up. He would meet with the local travel agent, their counterpart, who would handle the incoming guests, to work out the costs and percentages of the expenses. When they were in Bikaner, their travel agent host suggested they drive to the Karni Mata Mandir, which housed over twenty thousand black rats that devotees fed and worshiped, but neither Surya nor Damyanti had the stomach for it.

It was on one such travel that Surya first strayed; he was in a beautiful heritage property in Chikmaglur and the hotel manager had invited the owner of the property to have dinner with Surya. She had accompanied her father for the dinner and was chatty and flirtatious. She reminded him so much of his own wife, with the exception that she showed a keen interest in what he said, her pupils dilating just a little, indicating her involvement in the conversation. The next day, he left to return home, the hymen of loyalty that existed in his marriage broken. At first, he was ashamed and devastated at his weakness and transgression, wondering how he would face Damyanti. He knew that his wife read him like a book, so he was sure his crime would be discovered the moment he entered his home, but his fears were unfounded. That night, he reached out to make love to Damyanti, he rolled to her side of the bed and put his arm around her, but she sleepily said, "Let me sleep, Surya. Not today." When he persisted, she removed his hand from her body and said, "It's been a long day."

He tried again later that week and finally, on the weekend, she succumbed to his advances. As Surya entered her, he looked at her face, expecting to see passion, but he found her eyes dull and expressionless. He tried to kiss her, but as he put his lips on hers, she would not yield to let his tongue enter her mouth. Surya looked at the lifeless eyes, which showed no pleasure and he withdrew; Damyanti asked, "What happened?" He grimaced and said, "Nothing, just one of those days."

Their sex life dwindled to rare occasions; Surya would rather not have his self-esteem insulted; he preferred not to remember the deadpan eyes during their last encounter. It also gave him a reason to overcome the guilt that would arise with subsequent infidelities, although he knew within himself that it was just a justification for an act of disloyalty. Slowly, their relationship shifted from husband and wife to two people living in the same house, politely, respectfully but definitely as two distinct individuals.

It was around his eleventh wedding anniversary that he got the same dream again but this time around it was even stranger. He had not had alcohol the night before, so he was now sure it was not the whiskey talking. This time, he could see the idol more clearly, he was not sure if it was a just polished idol or a Shivling, for it was not a traditional lingam that he envisaged. The androgynous voice said, *I have been waiting for you, Surya. Why have you not come?* And then like the last time, the tone became a little more demanding as it reiterated, *I AM WAITING FOR YOU, SURYA.*

Surya sat up in bed and found himself sweating lightly, despite the cool air-conditioning. *It was just a dream,* he tried to reason with himself as he reached out for the water jar on his bedside, but he knew he was lying to himself; he did not believe it was just a dream, he was certain it was a message intended for him. After sipping his water, he tried to sleep, but the words from the dream echoed in his head and he lay in bed, playing absent-mindedly with the hair on his stomach, wondering who had sent this message, unable to sleep. He wondered why the message was sent to him for he was never a big believer in the gods, visiting temples occasionally, primarily to appease his parents or humor his wife and in-laws. He got out of bed as silently as he could and went into the study; he took his iPad and started to search for famous black idols. He decided not to mention it to Damyanti this time or anyone else, for it seemed too irrational and absurd.

The next morning, he asked Damyanti if she would like to visit Balaji and she agreed to accompany him. Tushar from their office had made perfect arrangements and they climbed the 3550 steps in less than four hours, chanting *Govinda Govinda Govinda*; they got sufficient time for a very satisfactory 'darshan' but Surya was disappointed for when he saw the statue of Balaji, he was awed and duly respectful, but he knew this was not the statue that had spoken to him in his dreams.

A couple of months later, in October, Damyanti and Surya combined their annual vacation with a work visit. They needed to check out a boutique hotel in Udaipur to add to their listing, so they decided to stay there and experience the city of lakes. Before they left, Surya suggested that they visit the famous temple of Nathdwara, so Tushar was left to make his impeccable arrangements. They went early morning to the Shreenathji Temple. They stood in the separate lines for men and women and soon found themselves inside, jostled and pushed, the faithful chanting *Jai Shri Krishna*. Surya was mesmerized by the large eyes of the black idol, they were hypnotic, but he knew that this was not the Lord who had beckoned him.

The couple returned to Mumbai; it would be a hectic period. The winters were always busy for them at work and they would work long hours. The dream would not trouble Surya; it remained in the recess of his mind as life resumed normally for both of them. He continued to visit his parents on Sunday for lunch and his mother-in-law for dinner on Tuesdays after work. One Friday night, as Surya and Jaideep sat in his living room, with their drinks in their hands, Jaideep asked Surya, "What are you dreaming of, my friend? You don't seem to be here today. Is everything okay?"

Surya stared at Jaideep, his words had somehow touched him especially after the drinks, the words 'dream' and 'friend' that Jaideep had used in his sentence got him drifting by word association. He decided to break his resolve and speak to Jaideep about the two dreams he had had. He was relieved that Jaideep did not smirk and instead was understanding and sympathetic. Surya proceeded to explain his visits to the temples of Tirupati and Nathdwara and Jaideep nodded his head, "Why did you not mention it to me earlier? Your dream is from Shiva and you are visiting other temples."

Surya stared at Jaideep, it was so obvious and he had overlooked such a basic point. He sat there with his mouth slightly open. His parents had worshiped Krishna and they had a small blue statue in their little temple at home; his wife prayed to another version of Krishna in their house, so Surya had failed to make the connection with Shiva in his dream in spite of all the glaring symbology.

"You don't have to go looking for Shiva and the black statue," said Jaideep, "you cannot do it for there are millions of them. Let the voices themselves guide you to where you need to go, don't rush it."

"Why did I hear the voices?" said Surya, relieved to be able to discuss this vivid dream with someone, "I mean why not someone else?"

"There are so many forces at play that we have no knowledge of, so how can anyone answer why you and not someone else? Don't get bothered about it, take it in your stride, and listen to what it has to say to you."

*****

The following October, a few months before their twelfth wedding anniversary, Damyanti and Surya went to a lesser-known resort in Orissa. Their project was doing well and Beej had suggested that they tie-up with some locations in Orissa. "It's a state that has been lesser-visited and there are some remarkable places there," he said. "I will not recommend Araku in nearby Andhra as it has very little infrastructure but there is this unknown seaside town called Gopalpur-on-sea that's located on the Bay of Bengal."

"Gopalpur-on-sea?" asked Damyanti, "Beej bhai, it does not even sound like an Indian city."

"It's a small town," said Beej, "but it has a stunning beach with an ancient lighthouse. There's plenty for us to market to our clients; there's the Chilka Lake close by, which has dolphins in it, and there are scenic drives. For the kids, there is a water park too."

"Are there any hotels in that town that are worth living in?" asked Surya, for he knew that there would probably be no habitable dwelling that would be acceptable for the high-ticket client.

"Actually, there is," said Beej smiling. "I believe there is a hotel, with old-world charm, built by an Italian, maybe a hundred years ago. You'll love it and it will fit in perfectly with our clients' requirements. Tushar can do the fact-finding and bookings. I suggest you try it out."

Damyanti and Surya decided to visit Gopalpur-on-sea and stay there for three days, exploring the surrounding areas and taking their time off before the busy season started at work. When they arrived, they were taken aback, for the property was luxurious and better than what they had expected. The hotel manager was expecting them, and he stood at the entrance to welcome them; they were after all commercially important guests that could help promote the hotel. He personally escorted them around the property and gave them the suite overlooking the sea. It was near the secluded swimming pool, surrounded by lush vegetation; there were a few Balinese gazebos with sundeck chairs in and around the pool.

"Beej bhai was right, it will be perfect," said Damyanti gaily, "I cannot believe this resort exists in the middle of nowhere. I wonder why we have never even heard of it before!.."

They stepped into the vast lawns beyond the reception and walked toward the beach. She was wearing comfortable striped palazzos, a thin silver anklet on her bare ankles, and a wide straw hat. She walked lazily in her sandals next to her husband; his hand rubbed against hers and he gently took them into his own hands and entwined his fingers in them. They were always very gentle with each other in the October holidays, the unspoken and unacknowledged birth month of their unborn child. Surya thought he had moved on but recognized that the baby had done its mission of bringing the parents together.

They sat under the umbrellas set up by the hotel, overlooking the beach below, sipping chai and munching biscuits with it.

"This is delicious."

"It should be," said Surya smiling, his sunglasses reflecting the sea, "One of the online reviewers had mentioned that this is the best chai served in India. I must get some *jhalmuri* for us to try out too. They have a counter here that specially prepares it for evening tea."

As Surya walked to get the packets of freshly mixed jhalmuri, Damyanti looked at him. *He has matured so well,* she thought to herself, *he is looking so good.* She remembered her father's words to her; one day as Damyanti and her father sat for office lunch privately in his cabin (as they did each afternoon), he had casually mentioned Surya to her. "He is a good boy," he said gently, "you should be kinder with him." She had tossed her hair and looked angrily at her father and said, "I am very nice with him." She had been so firm that her father understood not to broach on the topic further.

That evening they walked on the beach; they examined the towering lighthouse next to the hotel and Surya climbed into a shipping boat, which was on at its base. He gave his hand out to Damyanti, who squealed, but climbed into the old sailing craft, and they stood together facing the sea, his hand holding hers. At night, they changed into smart casuals and walked to the old-fashioned bar near the lobby. It had wood-paneled walls and leather chairs; they sat relaxed, their whiskey glasses in hand, munching the peanuts and talking about the property and the beautiful time at the beach.

After a couple of drinks, Damyanti giggled a little more than normal and started flirting with her husband, who smiled at her, happy to see this side, a facet normally reserved for her childhood friends.

"Let's spend tomorrow in the pool," she said coquettishly to him.

"Aren't we supposed to explore the lake tomorrow?" he asked.

That night, it was she who made the move in bed, and Surya happily obliged; they made love with animal passion and it felt a little like the old times when they were newly married.

That night was the third and last time that he got the same dream.

It was vivid; Surya knew he was dreaming but yet felt that he was awake and transported into another reality. The same hazy black stone idol but the voice simply said, *I will be waiting for you. I know you will come. I will be waiting for you.*

This time Surya did not wake up in a panic as the previous two times; he sat up in bed calmly and put on his underwear. He used the blue light of his phone to navigate himself to the living room of the suite. He looked at the time, it was just past 5 a.m. His sleep gone, he sat cross-legged on the sofa wondering what to do next; he opened the browser of his phone and started to look for prominent temples nearby, with black idols. The results of the search were compelling: the Jagannath Temple at Puri.

Surya stared at the picture of the temple and knew that he had to visit it; at that time of dawn, his mind was very aware, very awake, his thoughts were crystal clear and there was no shred of doubt in his mind that he should go to Puri, although he knew it was a Krishna temple and not a Shiva one. He checked the routing and it showed a clean drive of just over four hours. Surya rose from the sofa and stealthily walked to the desk to plan; first, he had to come up with a good excuse to tell Damyanti. He didn't want to expound about his dream to her for he was unsure about her reaction; he decided to tell her that he was making this one-day visit as part of the neighborhood exploration.

Secondly, he had to make travel arrangements. He wanted to leave in a couple of hours and it would be impossible to call Tushar in their office for help, so he decided to speak to the hotel team for assistance. On the side of the table, there was a plate of '*mithai*' with a visiting card of the hotel manager who had shown them around when they checked in. He took the card carefully and squinted to read it. Mr Pankaj, the manager's name was legible and below it was the mobile number in italics. Surya sent the manager a text apologizing for the early hour of the message and asking if a car could be urgently arranged for him. He got a reply sooner than he expected: *a car could most certainly be arranged; it would be a pleasure.*

A third problem surfaced in Surya's mind. He had only visited two temples in the past, both with Damyanti, and their office had arranged entry to the main shrine for darshan. He knew as a layman it would be difficult to get a proper entry, it may be a wait of several hours without any prior connection to smoothen the process.

As he mulled over this, he remembered Jaideep's words; hadn't he said something about 'let the voice in the dream guide you and not to get too worked up about it'? He decided to go along with the flow and trust the voice to sort the problem of darshan. Otherwise, he reasoned with himself, it was not meant to happen and he would simply come back. Chilka Lake was en route and if the temple visit was unsuccessful, he could easily visit the lake as part of the work exploration on his return.

Surya kissed Damyanti on the forehead. "I will try to return in time for the chai at the beach," he said. He reached the lobby and the manager was waiting for him; next to him stood an elderly man.

"Thank you, Pankajji," Surya said to the manager, "for arranging transportation for me at such short notice."

"It is nothing," said the manager modestly, and turning to the elder gentleman standing beside him, "This is Ravi, he is our most trusted driver. He will take you to Puri and back."

Surya looked at the driver and asked, "Raviji, how long will it take us to reach?"

Working in the travel trade, he had got used to respectfully adressing everyone he met by their first name whether it was the luggage attendant or the driver; he saw it really worked wonders.

Ravi looked at his watch and said, "It will take us about four hours. There is not much traffic either."

The manager smiled and told Surya, "It is a very scenic drive along the lake. You will not even realize how the time will pass by."

He looked at the driver and said, "Don't forget to show Suryaji the dolphins at Chilka."

Pankaj escorted Surya to the car and said, "Don't worry about anything. Raviji is our most experienced driver. He knows the ways and has done this round trip several times with the guests. He will stop at a nice place for lunch too. Have a good darshan at the temple.

I wish madam could also accompany you, but I know she has meetings with my team today."

Thus, Surya drove off to the large temple in Puri, the temple that did not allow non-Hindus to enter, raising the pique and ire of the British during their rule, a temple that created awe and gave rise to the English word 'juggernaut'.

Meanwhile in Puri, in the temple that Surya was going to visit, Tapovan waited in the parking lot. He had stopped doubting the veracity of dreams many years ago and this time the dreams were too real to be ignored. He stood patiently as his name indicated and waited. He had been christened Tapovan by the other priests of the temple when they had inducted him in their fold, for it meant a thick forest of spirituality based on the level of penances that he would do. He had come wandering to Puri, maybe thirty years ago as a tourist and he had visited the temple. When he had entered the sanctum to view the three deities, he saw a priest in the inner sanctum near the statues staring at him. The eyes of the priest would not leave the visitor and when he left the sanctum to go outside, he saw the priest running toward him. It was the head priest and he came up to him and asked him his name.

"My name is Tapan," he had said. The priest had looked up at the sun, his palm forming a visor above his eyes and said, "Your name means the sun. It is not so often that the Lord of the Skies visits us. I am sure that you will shine just as brightly for us here as you do up there."

Tapan had wondered what the priest was talking about. Little did he know that the temple would soon become his home and that one day he would be one of the servitors himself. During his early days at the temple, he had heard others question the head priest about the new uninitiated entrant and why he should be allowed in this post without proper knowledge of the scriptures. "Is he even a Brahmin?" one had asked. "He does not know Sanskrit," said another.

"He will learn it all," the head priest had said. "I have been told about his arrival in a dream," said the head priest quietly, with such finality and that answer seemed to be sufficient for all of them. Tapan had not understood the statement of a dream at that time but he had started penance and practicing austerities to justify his presence in the temple, to compensate for his inexperience, to prove his competence to the head priest who had so much faith in him. He never knew that his visit to the temple would lead him into a life of priesthood, it seemed so outlandish and bizarre when he thought about it. That was so many years ago but it all came back to Tapovan as he stood waiting in the parking lot for the stranger. It was now, after so many decades, that he had comprehended what the head priest had meant when he said he had dreamed about Tapan, and he now understood that the head priest had waited for him so many years ago as he was waiting for this man to come.

But luckily for Tapovan, he would not have to initiate this stranger. His role was much simpler.

In the car, while going toward Puri, Surya realized that he knew little about the temple and asked the driver for information.

"The temple is very special," said the driver to Surya, looking at him through the rear-view mirror, "There are many inexplicable things there."

Surya was surprised; with furrows in his forehead and genuine interest, he leaned forward and asked the driver, "Like what things?"

The driver pulled over near a stall and asked, "Would you like some tea?"

Surya knew this was an offer not to be refused as probably the elderly driver needed a cup of hot chai himself. "I would love a cup, Raviji," said Surya, "as long as you give me company and have some tea too."

Ravi poured the tea in a saucer and blew on it like Surya would have done years ago. He slurped it noisily and said, "There is a divine force at the temple. Hundreds of scientists have come from far away, even from *Amreeka* but have not been able to explain it."

Surya knew that a lot of the tales were just word of mouth fables and exaggerated stories but nonetheless he was interested in what the elderly gentleman had to say. "Do tell me more," he said gently.

Encouraged, the driver said, "Well for one, the temple casts no shadow. It stands on such a blessed spot that there is no shadow of the structure at any time of the day, and mind you, the temple is nearly as tall as a forty-storied building."

He glanced at Surya and saw him looking suitably interested and continued, "Every day the priest climbs the temple steeple from outside, forty floors high, without any ropes or scaffolding to change the flag. This has been going on since the temple was built. They say, if it is not done, then the temple will have to shut down for many years. What is more, the flag that is on the temple does not fly in the direction of the wind."

Seeing Surya looking puzzled, he went on to explain, "Normally a flag flies in the same direction as the wind does, but on this temple, it flies in the opposite direction. And next to the flag is an iron disk. People say it is a copy of Vishnuji's Sudarshan Chakra and weighs hundreds of kilograms. How they got it up so high in those days without any machines is a mystery. What is more, you can see the disk from everywhere in the city and it always seems to be facing you, whichever angle you see it from. Such is the power of the temple."

They finished the chai and resumed their journey; Surya could not help but fall in love with the scenic drive along the lake, water birds flying and thick green foliage all over. Time passed by quickly as predicted by the manager and soon they reached the city of Puri and the temple complex. Ravi stopped the car at the parking lot. "We can go no further from here," he said, "I will help you with the entrance tickets to it and get you a guide but I will have to wait here."

"You take your time and have a good darshan, I will be here only," said Ravi and then added quickly, "I remembered one more thing about the temple. The gods of the temple like their silence and peace so once you enter any of the four doors to the temple, you stop hearing the sound of the sea completely. You can hear it at the doorway but it completely fades off as soon as you step in. So much so, there is no plane or bird that flies over the temple." Surya looked up to the sky and could not see a bird and so he opened his eyes a little to show amazement and nodded his head. "See sir, that is the temple there. You can see the disk on top, the one I told you about earlier, is facing us." Surya looked up and nodded again and then said, "Let me go inside." They exchanged mobile numbers. Surya took a photo of the car number plate and together, they walked to the ticket counter. They saw an elderly priest, thin and emaciated, but with a glow on his face, his bald head shining with a fringe of white hair at the sides, dressed in white robes approaching them.

"Do you wish to go to the temple?" he asked them.

Surya stared at the stranger, wondering what to answer when Ravi spoke up. "We will buy tickets and go the official way."

Ravi turned toward Surya and said softly, conspiratorially, "This temple complex is full of touts so you have to be careful."

Tapovan looked at Surya gently and smiled a peaceful smile, "What is your name, son?"

"I am Surya."

Tapovan was startled and then smiled, and he repeated the action that the head priest had done many years ago with him; he turned his head upwards and used his hand to form a visor and said, "The temple has always and will always welcome the sun. Allow me to take you inside to see the statues."

Surya looked back at the driver and said, "Raviji, it's okay. I will go with the priest. I will meet you here."

Tapovan led Surya to the buggies parked nearby; they were meant for the aged and important guests. The driver did a chaste namaste to the priest, bowing down sycophantly to touch the hem of Tapovan's white dhoti. They reached the main complex of the temple, about a kilometer away and Surya was whisked off through a private entrance into a dark passage. "This will lead us to the statues themselves," whispered Tapovan. When they reached the inner sanctum, Surya was dumbstruck when he saw the three idols as they were not what he expected. For one, they were larger than what he imagined they would be, nearly eight feet tall, with disproportionately large eyes, no legs or ears, painted in tribal fashion, looking like caricature art. It was the black statue that caught Surya's attention, it was not the one who he had dreamed of, but the round painted eyes stared at him and Surya found himself getting hypnotized as he focused on them.

Tapovan said, "Have you found what you were looking for?"

Surya found his mouth dry and his lips pursed, unable to answer. Finally, he mustered the strength and dumbly shook his head. In a hoarse voice, he said, "I am looking for a Shiva lingam and Jagannath is a representation of Vishnu."

Tapovan held Surya's hand and said, "The Lord of Jagannath is neither Vishnu nor Shiva. He just is. The Jains claim he is a *teerthankara* and thus give importance to the twenty-two steps leading to the temple, the Buddhist assert the tooth of Buddha was in the relics of the idols, the tantrics insist that the statues have all the symbology required to be theirs. The idols are mentioned in the Rig Vedas and at the same time, the local tribes claim them as theirs."

"So, these statues are really old, then?" asked Surya, unable to remove his gaze from the idols.

"They are supposed to be coming down from another era, by the gods themselves," said Tapovan; Surya turned to see if he was serious and realized the old man meant every word. "However, the statues are changed every few years, a fresh set of idols are made from the neem trees and four of us priests supervise the transfer of the soul from the old statues to the new."

Surya was surprised and asked, "What happens to the old statues?"

"They are buried in the graveyard of statues in the complex itself," said Tapovan. Just then another priest came up to Tapovan and did a chaste namaste. "Who is this gentleman and what is he doing in the inner sanctum?" asked the younger priest looking at Surya.

"He is Surya and he appeared to me in a dream," said Tapovan unabashedly. The younger priest brought his palms together and closed his eyes in a small prayer and turned to Surya and smiled at him, "Welcome, brother."

Later Surya asked Tapovan after the younger priest had left, "What is this dream you talk about and why would he believe it?"

"This temple was built because of a dream. Dreams are important here and all of us, who serve the Lord of Jagannath, know the language of dreams."

Surya looked at him, his eyes narrowing, "Since you understand the dialects of dreams, I need to talk to you about mine," he said.

"We will have time once we leave the inner sanctum," said Tapovan, "but for now, use this time to worship the Lord who has called you."

Surya looked outwards from inside at the outer sanctum where the worshippers gather and saw hordes of devotees a few meters in front of him, crushed together, their bodies mangled, their faces full of devotion, some with their heads bowed in deference, being pushed and guided for a few minutes of darshan. Some had come far for these few minutes, and he indeed realized his fortune of being inside the inner sanctum, up close with the three lords.

As they walked out down the steps of the main entrance, Tapovan stopped Surya on the fourth step from the bottom. "Be careful of the third step," he said, "do not step on the black stone."

Surya walked carefully, gingerly side-stepping the embedded black stone. He looked at Tapovan quizzically who smiled and said, "Each of these twenty-two steps has a name and a significance. But it is Yama who embedded this stone on the third step. Do you know who Yama is?"

Surya sighed deeply and said slowly, "Yes, my wife and I have met him briefly. He came for my unborn child." His face twisted and became small, his eyes misted and he tried not to cry. He wondered why he had said it and realized that it was a chapter in his mind that was not as closed as he had thought it was.

He collected himself and asked, "But how is Yama connected to Jagannath?"

Tapovan took the support of Surya's arm for the last two steps, but Surya suspected the old man was actually bracing him. "It is a long story and it starts with Yama. Everything always starts and ends with Yama."

They sat on a stone ledge and Tapovan spoke, "The story goes back to a time when Vishnuji came to earth in the form of Rama. When that period of time was coming to an end, Vishnuji manifested himself as a blue gem, called the Indranil Mani. This blue stone rested under a banyan tree, near the shores of the sea, pulsating with divine energy, its blue aura pervading the surrounding.

The Indranil Mani attracted everyone toward it and whoever saw it would get liberation for they had come in contact with the Lord. This instant *moksh* disturbed the role of Yama, the Lord of Death. He took the blue gem and buried it deep within the earth.

Eons passed, literally thousands of years. Krishnaji, the next avatar of Vishnuji came to the Earth. At the same time, there was a king called Indradyumna, a great devotee of Vishnuji. He had been told that there was a statue emanating blue light, in a hidden cave, worshiped by the tribal folk. It took him years to track the cave but when he finally reached the spot, full of excitement and anticipation, the statue had vanished.

On the day of Krishna Bhagwan's death, the king had a dream, 'Come to me,' the voice said, 'I will be waiting for you at Bankimuhan.'"

On the mention of the king's dream, Surya sat up, as if a bolt of electricity shot through him. The hair on his arms began to rise and his breath grew heavy. It was eerie that his dream was so similar to the king's.

Tapovan continued, "The king and his soldiers rushed to the spot and found a log from the neem tree, floating there, an alluring luminescence glowing from it, filling the surrounding with blueness. They took the divine log but now the king needed an architect who could build a temple worthy of the log, he needed a sculptor who would carve the image of the Lord on the log. Through a series of dreams, he managed to get a celestial architect as well as a sculptor and thus we have the divine temple of the Lord of the Universe."

"Now I understand why you said earlier that there is a great value of dreams at this temple," said Surya slowly. He glanced at his watch and knew he should be returning back soon so he could keep his date with Damyanti but he had so many questions.

"Why is the statue so incomplete? It does not have any arms or legs" he asked, "especially since it was created by divine intervention."

"That is yet another story," said Tapovan, "but I see you need to get back, so ask me what you were asking me inside, what is it that you need to know about your dream?"

Surya did not know where to begin, so he simply said, "I too had a dream and it was Shiva. The voice called me but I do not know where to go."

Tapovan looked at the sky and sighed. It was time. "Maybe, then you need to go to the city of Shiva and seek out the person calling you."

"And which is that city of Shiva?" asked Surya

"Varanasi," said Tapovan. He was relieved; he had performed his duty as he had dreamed; he had led the seeker to Varanasi. Tapovan smiled, his dream was fulfilled and it was time to get back to his temple duties.

"Let me drop you to the car," he said gently, leading the way, "It is time to go back now. I send you with all my blessings, son. Seek and you shall find, for you have been called."

They reached the parking lot and they found the driver patiently waiting.

"Can you get me back in time for tea and jhalmuri," asked Surya to the driver, for he was impatient to meet Damyanti. The driver looked at his watch and said, "I think we will make it."

Tapovan turned to leave Surya; he closed his eyes and said a quick prayer to Lord Jagannath, "Help him, my Lord, and let him meet Yama in peace."

CHAPTER 3

HOW RAJAT CAME TO VARANASI

"Logic will take you from A to B. Imagination will take you everywhere."

—Albert Einstein

Rajat stood at the receptionist's desk at the Taj Ganges hotel in Varanasi, waiting to check out. He wondered why they were so slow to give him the invoice copy, which the hospital needed; he leaned on the desk and said, "Please can you do it quickly? I am a doctor and an invitee by the Government and cannot keep waiting." The boy at the reception desk looked at him and smiled, did a slow namaste and said, "Yes Doctor *saab*, we are processing the bill."

"I do not think I have to pay anything," said Rajat, a bit impatiently, "It is being paid by the UP Government."

The boy behind the desk smiled again, unhurriedly rose to check a folio, and then attended a call, with no signs of speeding up. Rajat knew that he needed to be calm; he had been in Varanasi for a day on work and had realized that Einstein had got it right, time was relative, and it definitely seemed to move slower in this city.

He had felt important when Dr Mehrotra, the head of the department, and his mentor, had nominated him to be the delegate from their department of neurosciences to visit the city. The Chief Minister of the State of Uttar Pradesh had declared that Varanasi was going to be the hub for medical facilities and tourism. It was the city that the Prime Minister of the country had won his election from and many things had been promised. A large area had been set aside to build hospitals. The buildings were already coming up and the Government had invited representatives from leading hospitals to help set up state-of-the-art facilities in the ancient city of Varanasi.

"Are you sure there is no room available for the next two days?" asked Rajat to the tardy receptionist.

The boy stopped processing Rajat's bill and opened a new window on his computer to check the reservations. Rajat sighed, knowing the distraction meant a further delay in his checkout procedure and he should have waited for the receptionist to have completed his earlier task before mentioning another. The boy stared at the computer screen and said, "We are all sold out, sir." He saw the impatience on Rajat's face and said, "Doctor *saab*, please sit on the sofas and I will come and give you the printout. There is no payment to be made, but we need your signature."

Rajat sat on the sofa, wondering if he could yet make an excuse and go home for the weekend instead of staying on for two days more in this God-forsaken city. *What will I even do,* he thought to himself, *and now I have to change hotels?*

Nayana, his wife and he had gone for dinner to Rajat's mentor, Dr Mehrotra's house about a month ago. Dr Mehrotra, the senior doctor, was so flamboyant, suave and sophisticated that it was often said that his patients got infatuated by him and probably those were the same reasons for Rajat to feel slightly intimidated by him. His wife, too, was charming and that evening, at dinner at their house, she looked bewitching in a saree, the spaghetti straps of her blouse revealing her flawless skin with her well made-up face, manicured hands and her straight, ironed hair adding to her allure. They would invite Rajat and his wife for dinner once every six months since he got married and it meant a lot to the young doctor; it was an honor for him to go for dinner to Dr Mehrotra's house. Rajat had been surprised and relieved to see how well Nayana got along with the senior doctor's wife. At the last dinner, Dr Mehrotra spoke about taking a break by oneself, he had been so passionate about his solo holidays that Rajat felt that he was missing some vital experience. Dr Mehrotra spoke about his experiences when he stayed in a tiny village in Spain by himself or another one in the mountains. He had turned to Rajat and said, "Why don't you stay on in Varanasi for a couple of days after the meetings. That will be a perfect place to get some me-time. It is very important for a doctor, especially one in our department, to get a small break now and then".

Rajat had agreed for this two-day holiday all by himself enthusiastically but as the time had come near, he had dreaded it, wondering what he would do alone. His ego would not let him cancel the holiday plan and Nayana too seemed happy for him and had not suggested he should abandon the trip. He also knew that Dr Mehrotra would look at him disappointedly and say, "Well, my boy, you need to get out of your comfort zone."

So, here he was, for two days, by himself. Nayana had booked a charming boutique hotel, overlooking the riverfront, since rooms at the Taj were not available for his extended stay.

He sat on the sofa when he got a phone call from his wife.

"Have you checked out already?" she asked Rajat.

"I am waiting for the invoice," he said, "they are very slow here."

"I am so excited that you are doing this small break on your own. Remember what Dr Mehrotra had said, you need to let yourself go in such a vacation."

"I will try," said Rajat, trying to sound excited but was unconvincing, even to himself.

"There will be many temples and gods," said Nayana, and Rajat could feel her smiling at the other end, "Hear their stories with one ear and let it out through the other if it bothers you. Don't get worked up about it."

Rajat smiled; his wife knew him too well and always took care of the little things, "Don't worry," he said, "I will try and be a good tourist."

He paused and then added, "You probably do not know but I have two reasons to believe that God may just exist."

"What?" said Nayana incredulously, "I cannot believe you just said that. I should have recorded it for your mother to hear. Let me guess, one of them is your daughter, what is the second?"

"The only two reasons that may lead me to believe in God," said Rajat, very seriously and slowly (he wondered if the speed of Varanasi was affecting him too, in just one day of being here), "are one, that you came into my life. That has to be an act of God, for I truly am lucky to have you as my wife, and two, that I have this profession, which is what I always wanted."

Nayana trilled, "Rajat that is the most romantic thing you have said to me in the eleven years of our marriage. I was sure you would say it was our daughter."

"Nayana, how often have I explained that our daughter may be a miracle to you or a gift from God, but I am a scientist, a doctor, and for me, it is simply an act between man and woman, a sperm and an ova that made it happen," said Rajat, a little loudly, unabashed that someone may hear for he knew he had said something scientific and had nothing to be ashamed of.

On the other end, Nayana smiled, her husband was always so logical and correct.

"I will hang up now," said Rajat, "for the receptionist has finally got my checkout papers."

Nayana sat on her bed, thrilled at what her husband had told her. She was devoted to him. She put her feet up on the bed, picked up the photo frame from the bedside table, a wedding picture of Rajat and her looking so young and naïve. She remembered her initial days of marriage and living with the doctor and his parents.

*****

Mrinalini, Rajat's mother, sat with the new bride one afternoon when both the doctors were away at work. Nayana had cooked lunch and the two women sat on the dining table to eat it.

Nayana was slightly nervous about whether her mother-in-law would find a lapse in the food she had prepared but she told herself not to fall in the traditional role and to be confident of her cooking. After all, making her mother-in-law larger than life in her mind was also doing both women a disfavor.

Mrinalini served herself a second helping of the vegetables cooked by Nayana. She looked up at the young woman and smiled, "This is delicious."

Nayana smiled, a slight relief flooding her, in spite of her earlier resolve and she said shyly, "Rajat loves the food you cook. I must learn the recipes."

Mrinalini could not help but feel her heart swell up at the praise but she controlled the feeling and instead said, "I am around to cook the old, familiar food of his childhood. I am glad you are cooking different things and flavors for Rajat; he will get to try out new dishes."

After lunch, they sat and Mrinalini started on a few topics that had been playing on her mind; she knew Nayana was as an intelligent girl but she also knew that what she was going to say could be misunderstood so she broached the topic gently.

"I don't want us to have the typical problems faced by daughters-in-law and mothers-in-law. I do not have a daughter of my own, and I am happy to have got one now that you have come to the house," she said slipping Nayana's hand into her own. "We both have a common man that we love, Rajat is my son, and he is also your husband," she continued.

Nayana did not know how to answer, so she just nodded her head for there was nothing wrong with what the elder lady was saying. She could feel her affection, and so she smiled and murmured, "That is true, we both love him."

"I will not interfere between you both," said Mrinalini, "and I will not expect you two to spend too much time with us. You are young and you need time with each other. I am glad he has found a partner who understands the importance of his profession. Have new experiences together, explore new areas, and make memories together. His father and I are always there as support."

"I know how valuable his work is and I plan to support him on it fully as you have done to Daddyji," said Nayana.

Mrinalini smiled, "And that is why I will not teach you the recipes of his childhood. For he does not need another mother, he already has me. He needs a wife and he has you." She had said this line that she had wanted to deliver as smoothly as possible, without it coming across as a subtle warning. She looked at her daughter-in-law to see if it had been received badly, but she was relieved when Nayana looked back at her and smiled at her warmly, and gratefully.

They both asked the kitchen help for coffee and Mrinalini continued, "It is a wise woman who keeps her husband and family all well-knit together. Our husbands are busy doctors and they do not have time for petty matters of the household, so it is up to us to keep the harmony in the house. In our earlier apartment, we were very friendly with our neighbors, our doors remained opened for each other for most of the day. When the son of the household got married, we were part of the celebrations. However, it was sad to see the new marriage fail. The newlyweds loved their own mothers too much, and that took precedence over the love for each other."

Taking the last sip of coffee, Mrinalini rose. "I shall get back to my room," she said. Many thoughts whirred in her head. She was glad that Nayana was a gentle but clever woman, she would be able to handle her son. Rajat, she knew, was very intelligent, and with that intelligence came its own share of problems. He had always had fixed ideas since he was a child. He would protest when Mrinalini wanted to do her morning prayers, and so she would sit in the little temple room after he had left for school. "I don't like this useless worship of a statue," he would grumble and then argue about it incessantly, until Mrinalini would sigh and agree with him, exhausted from the chastisement. But he would drag on a topic, giving various logical reasons, challenging the dogmas of faith. As he grew older, he would be bitter when he would read articles on religious intolerance or prejudice, whether it was the Bamiyan Buddhas being blown up in Afghanistan or the temple and mosque debate in North India. "I hate religion and how it is practiced as it turns people into bigots," he would argue, "I would like to give them a poison to eradicate all people who are fanatics," not realizing that his stand itself was fanatical, in the other extreme.

Mrinalini lay in bed for an afternoon snooze and remembered a parent-teacher meeting at Rajat's school when he was younger. All the teachers had praised him, for he was an exceptionally bright student, focused and would dedicatedly walk on the path he had chosen. He knew that he wanted to be a doctor, like his father, ever since he was young. He could not remember a time when he wanted to be anything else. His class teacher had said something to Mrinalini, who had always attended the meetings alone as her husband was at the hospital. Mrinalini remembered the exact words, even after so many years. "Rajat is an ideal student," the teacher had said, "but we should be careful for him." Mrinalini's ears had pricked up, hanging on to each word that the teacher said. "Everything is black and white for Rajat," the teacher had continued, "he must learn to see the shades of gray in between as well. He will have to learn to walk on the via media." Mrinalini had looked puzzled and had asked, "What is via media? I am sorry I did not understand." The teacher gently said, "It means Rajat will have to learn to compromise. He is young yet, Mrs Baheti, but you and I have lived life to know that you cannot walk on the extreme. Life will teach bitter lessons. Besides, at work and also with his spouse, he will have to learn to walk between the extremes, to adjust, to accept, to be less judgmental." Mrinalini was drifting into sleep; she had known this about her son all long; *he is like his father* she thought, *Nayana is a wise woman, she has to manage and has a lot cut out for her to handle.*

Nayana adjusted well into the household, easier than what had been anticipated by Mrinalini, much to her relief. Nayana loved her husband dearly and respected his role as a doctor. When she was a young girl, she had seen her grandfather suffer from Parkinson's disease. Her father would visit the neurologist as he was the first caregiver. Over time, their doctor had become almost revered. She would see her father touching the doctor's feet, sometimes with tears of anguish in his eyes, trying to resolve her grandfather's plight, and so Nayana developed this deep deference toward all doctors. When the marriage proposal came for Rajat, she was delighted that her husband-to-be was a neurologist, for she had pedestaled all doctors, especially those dealing with the brain. It did not matter that the young man wore spectacles, or that he had thinning hair already, or that he was a few years older than her. What did matter to her was that he helped people, with problems that other people could not deal with, with illnesses of the brain, like epilepsies, brain tumors and strokes and diseases like Alzheimer's and Parkinson's. She knew she would be a support to her husband-to-be, helping in whatever way to carry out the important task that he had set out to do. Over time, Rajat along with his father had started a private clinic and Nayana would handle a lot of the administration work.

In the initial period, Rajat was a gawky husband. He did not know how to show emotion but Nayana did not seem to mind. If his stomach was bad, and he had to eat light *khichdi*, then Nayana too would eat the same dish. "I like it," she would tell Mrinalini, who would coax her to eat the other food cooked. If he would come back late at night due to an emergency meeting at the hospital, once even at midnight, she would wait for him and heat the food so they could eat together. Mrinalini would chide her when they ate their lunch together, but Nayana would explain that she loved the young doctor and it was no compromise or sacrifice for her. Rajat was awkward in bed; he had had sex only a couple of times before he met Nayana when his college friends had coaxed him and had hired the services of a paid sex worker. His approach with Nayana was clinical and involved no foreplay, no passionate kissing. He bit her breasts in passion, he ejaculated in the condom and withdrew and rolled over. Instead of getting upset, Nayana realized something was amiss. Since this was her first experience with sex, she knew it was not the sensual communion that she heard about in hushed whispers and giggles with her friends. She did not wish to talk about it with anyone, so she bought a few guides and self-help books on the internet and would read them in the privacy of her room. Over the next few weeks, she started to introduce the concept of massage in the bedroom; at first on the pretext to relieve him from the stress of his work for she did not want him to get defensive or feel inadequate and slowly added sensual touches that Rajat found impossible to resist. One night, she said she had a backache and asked the inexperienced doctor to massage it and slowly she guided him from the books she had read, from her own instinct, from the woman she was and together they learned from each other, the primeval act, always known to man and woman. She left a book near the toilet and as expected, Rajat leafed through it while sitting on the pot. "Did you know this book says that some women can reach orgasm by nipple stimulation?" he said when he came out of the toilet. Not waiting for an answer, he said, "This book is very informative. Please keep it on my bedside and I will read it later."

Nayana slowly changed the products he used; *a man who helps so many people, needs someone to look after him*, she reasoned. She added a good deodorant and mouth wash, changed his razor blades as well as the ties he wore. Their love life blossomed but it was always built on the solid foundation of love, thereby sanctifying the union several times over.

At work too, it was Dr Mehrotra who brought about change in Rajat and his working style. Rajat was a fantastic doctor, but not a great communicator. There had been a few instances where Dr Mehrotra, the senior head of the neurosciences department, had intervened. He knew Rajat's father and he knew the young doctor was dedicated and very qualified, but he also realized that Rajat was not a people's person. He took him under his wing and slowly started to coach him on how to handle patients.

Dr Mehrotra would have Rajat sit in with him for some clients meeting so he could learn by observation. Once, they sat with a patient, who was suffering from a tumor in the brain, which would soon grow and affect the nerves, and the son asked whether they should use alternate medicines from Dharamsala. The son went on to explain, "These are special tablets that attack the tumor, made by a Tibetan doctor, he is a Buddhist monk. Maybe we should give his medicine a try." Dr Mehrotra looked toward Dr Rajat, asking him to reply. Rajat found himself enraged with the son's suggestion. He said, "Why don't you pluck leaves from the tree outside the hospital and feed him? They were planted by a monk too. You people do not realize how serious the matter is; we are trying chemo and every possible solution and you want to give roots and herbs without any medical evidence or scientific study. Do you know how many days the patient has?" The son looked down, embarrassed and crestfallen and Dr Mehrotra intervened, and said gently, "What Dr Rajat is saying is that while we doctors are doing the best to help the patient, you must try whatever you can, if you think it will help him. While we have no proven success cases with this alternate medicine by the Tibetan doctor, please do try, you never know if a miracle can happen, especially as the patient has only a few weeks. Let us all try the best options together as a team." Later, he explained to Rajat that bad news must always be imparted carefully and gently to the patients' families, that he must be tolerant with desperate clients and empathetic to their relatives.

On another occasion, when Rajat was consulting in his clinic, a patient wanted to use homeopathic medicines for his mother, who suffered from Alzheimer's disease. Rajat found himself getting angry but controlled his temper, just as his mentor had taught him. He wished he had learned this when he was in school for it would have saved him from many arguments with other students when he debunked ghosts and spirits on a camping trip or would mock their conspiracy theories as baseless and unscientific.

After a few years of the young doctor's marriage, Rajat's parents bought the neighboring flat and moved there. Nayana often had lunch with her mother-in-law and supervised a lot of the cleaning and grocery buying so they did not feel isolated, but it was also nice for the young couple to have the full house to themselves. Rajat grew busier than ever, he was in his mid-thirties and his practice and fame as a doctor kept growing and Nayana started to look after the household and later the clinic. She knew many other wives of doctors who grumbled and complained that their husbands were too busy and did not have time for the family; for Nayana, her husband was an agent of God, helping others and she tried to be the support to him that she had set out to be when she married him. She was carrying their child, and Mrinalini would spend time with her, insisting that she should eat on fixed times instead of waiting for her husband. Subtly, Mrinalini would slip in advice, in the garb of stories of other neighbors; Nayana knew the tales were a disguise to good-natured counsel, for her mother-in-law did not have the large number of varied neighbors that her stories indicated. One tale was about a neighbor whose wife and son treated him poorly. "Children behave toward the father as they see their mothers do. So, be careful how your child perceives the relationship between you and Rajat for he or she will emulate you subconsciously." Another time, it was about how an aged neighbor started ignoring her husband as they grew older and became more dependent on her son. "Remind me of this story," said Mrinalini, "if I land up leaning on Rajat instead of my own husband."

*****

Rajat left the Taj Ganges in the car that had been arranged for him and made his way to the new boutique hotel booked for him by Nayana. "How long will it take to get to Kailash Kothi?" he asked the driver.

"It depends on Mahadev, sir, we will reach when he wishes us to reach," said the driver.

"Who is Mahadev?" asked Rajat, perplexed.

The driver pointed upwards and said, "Mahadev, sir. Shivji," and added, "and also on the traffic. We have to go to a jetty and the hotel boat will take you to the hotel."

Rajat rolled his eyes in exasperation and said, "You mean I need to reach the hotel by boat? Is there no road there?"

"It is on the banks of Gangaji, in the old city, and the best way to get to the hotel will be by boat from the jetty, and it will be the quickest too."

At the hotel, as Rajat was checking in, he saw a man, very boyish in appearance, at the reception desk.

"I would like to book a boat ride on the Ganges," said the elfin man.

"I am afraid, Mr Amrit, the boat has been booked for a private ride," said the receptionist. Rajat wanted to check-in but he was aware that things cannot be pushed in Varanasi and one must let them go at their own pace. He looked at the name tag, and interjected to the receptionist, "Mr Sunil, I too would like a boat ride. Maybe, we can fix one boat for both of us."

The boyish man looked up and smiled at Rajat. He extended his hand and said, "Hello, I am Amrit. It will be convenient to share the boat."

Awkwardly, Rajat let go of his suitcase handle and stretched out his hand and said, "I am Dr Rajat Baheti, Neurologist." He was happy if he could piggyback on this boat ride for he had no clue what he was going to do or how he would fill his time in the next two days.

Sunil, the receptionist said, unhelpfully, "I am afraid that the hotel boat has been booked for a special guest. I will try and arrange for another one from one of the tour operators."

Just then, two men came by and Sunil rose. "Good morning, sir," he said, very dutifully.

"Good afternoon, Sunilji," said the man, who was obviously his boss, looking at his watch, "it is nearly two o'clock in the afternoon and you are wishing us good morning."

"Yes, yes, Mukulji," said Sunil hastily, "I meant good afternoon. We have arranged the private boat for Suryaji. At what time would you like to depart for the boat ride?"

Amrit stared at Surya and averted his glance for he did not want them to notice. *What a dish!* he thought to himself. Rajat in the meantime stepped forward and said, "I am Dr Rajat Baheti, Neurologist. I believe that the hotel boat has been booked by you for this afternoon. I was wondering if both of us could join in."

Mukul, the hotel manager fumbled and started to say something, but Surya smiled and said, "Yes it will be good to have company as I am all alone." He turned to the receptionist and said, "Please can you keep the boat ready for 4 p.m. departure?"

Chapter 4

Varanasi, Day 1 Afternoon: The Boat Ride on the River

"Sometimes even the wrong train takes us to the right destination."

Mukul came to drop the three of them to the pier. A man in the hotel uniform stood at the jetty, his hands together in the respectful namaste. "This is Prabodji," said Mukul. "He will accompany you on the boat and give you the history of each ghat. His knowledge of the stories of Varanasi is fascinating."

Surya and his companions looked appreciatively at Prabod who smiled and said, "Please do not hesitate to ask me anything. I will be happy to give you whatever little information I know."

Mukul turned to Prabod and said, "Please take special care," indicating Surya with his eyes, "I hope Sunilji has given you the chai and snacks for the guests." Prabod nodded and assisted the three of them on the boat. He introduced them to the boatman, a rotund balding man, seated at one end of the vessel. "This is Rajbirji," he said, "he is an experienced boatman and will take us for a long ride down the Ganges."

Amrit piped in at this moment, asking for the life jacket.

"It's not necessary," said Surya gently, "but I suppose it is safer if it makes you feel comfortable. I do not need one."

"I think I will wear it," said Amrit.

Prabod looked at Rajbir and said, "We have scheduled a two-hour boat ride. Suryaji and his friends have come to experience Gangaji." With a knowing glance, he added, "He is a special guest of the hotel."

The boat left the little hotel jetty and at a relaxed pace, as everything else in this city was, maneuvered in the direction of the water flow. They sailed for a few meters when Rajat pointed to the fire burning at a distance and asked, "Rajbirji, what is that ghat?"

Rajbir laughed, his belly moving up and down and said, "That is the *nabhi* of Kashi." Rajat noticed that the local residents preferred calling Varanasi by its traditional name, Kashi.

Seeing all three men looking blank, Prabod interjected, "Nabhi is the Hindi word for navel, belly button."

Rajbir then proceeded to explain, tucking the *paan* that he was chewing on the side of his mouth, "Someone has said that India is the navel of the world. In India, we say, Kashi is the navel of India. And when people come here, they ask us, what is the navel of Kashi? To those people we say, that ghat there, called the Manikarnika Ghat, is the navel of Kashi. We will go closer to it on the return journey."

"And why is it the navel of Varanasi or Kashi as you all call it?" asked Rajat.

Prabod started to explain, "In many ancient beliefs, the belly button is the seat of spirituality in a human being. It is the first point that develops on conception, linking the embryo to the mother's womb. All development takes place from there and all blood vessels and nerves are connected from that point in development. Spiritually too, it is the connecting point for a person from one lifetime to another."

Rajat was contemplating whether he should medically and scientifically explain to the boatman that there was nothing spiritual about the belly button but he decided against it.

Surya interrupted and said, "I have a private guide taking me to see the gulleys and ghats of Varanasi tomorrow. Why don't you guys join me? He will explain all about the Manikarnika Ghat too."

Rajat looked at him and smiled, "Thank you Surya, I would love to join and I will be happy to pay for my share too."

"That will not be necessary as it is paid by my office. I am here on a travel exploratory trip."

"What time do you plan on going?" asked Amrit, "for I am busy in the morning."

"I will be going to the Kashi Vishwanath temple in the morning, so I plan on doing the walking tour in the afternoon post-lunch."

"Then I too would like to join in, please," said Amrit. "I am busy in the morning so it's perfect for me. I am planning to do the evening *aarthi* at the main ghat. It is organized by the hotel free of cost you know."

Rajat said, "I will be going to the evening aarthi tomorrow evening as well. Will our walking tour end in time for the aarthi? Can we do the walk a little earlier?"

"We will be in time for the evening aarthi, don't worry," said Surya, "I will be going for the aarthi as well."

"I am free in the morning tomorrow. Can I join any one of you?" asked Rajat.

"I am sorry," said Amrit. "I have booked a private boat and am going to immerse the ashes of my mother in the holy waters."

"And I will be going to the temple but I need to go alone." Seeing their puzzled faces, Surya continued to explain, "While I have come on a business visit, I also have a personal agenda." He then continued speaking, not understanding why he was giving so much information, but unable to control himself, "I have come to seek Shiva. He appeared to me in a series of dreams and I think that I will finally meet him at the Kashi Vishwanath temple."

Before the others could react, Rajbir said, "Suryaji, you will not meet Shivji in the temple. You can skip going there."

Surya looked at him sharply and said, "What do you mean?"

"What he means is," said Prabod placatingly, "is that Mahadev is not restricted to the temple. In Kashi, He is everywhere. You will find Him on the ghats, you will find Him on the banks of the Ganges and you will find Him at the tea stall."

"And you will find Him at the ganja seller buying hash," added Rajbir the boatman, laughing at his own joke, his belly moving again. "Varanasi is the city of Shiva; He is all over the place. You do not need to go to the temple at all to meet Him."

"Go I must," said Surya, very definitively.

"Yes, maybe you should," said Prabod, "If Mahadev has called, then why not?"

Rajat sidled up next to Surya and said, "I said I was a neurologist when we met, so I can explain some things. There are many aspects to dreams and how they are related to the brain."

The boat was floating serenely down the river and far in the distance, they could see young boys playing cricket, their old bats held together by different tapes, the balls worn-out and battered. Further along, women were washing their household linen on the banks.

"I would love to know what science has to say about these dreams and visions," said Surya quietly. Amrit moved an inch closer too, indicating his interest as well.

"Our brains are divided into two hemispheres," said Rajat, "In the center of the brain, between the two hemispheres is a small gland. It's really small, a reddish-gray color, maybe the size of a pea," he said, showing the approximate size with his fingers. "It's called the pineal gland because of its pine cone shape. Its location is directly behind the forehead, in between the two eyebrows."

"Is that what we call the third eye?" said Amrit excitedly, "We concentrate at that point in yoga. In our chakra meditation too, it's the *Agaya* chakra, located in the brain, between the eyebrows, an energy center."

Rajat wanted to explain to him that medical science has found no evidence of these energy centers, chakras or a subtle body but he controlled himself. "That gland is indeed referred to as the third eye or even sometimes called the seat of the soul. It is responsible for many things." Rajat continued, "Earlier, it was thought to be only in charge of secreting melatonin, which controls sleep patterns and determines your body clock and jet lag. Light from the eyes is sent to the gland and it determines the melatonin secretion and thus makes you sleepy or awake. At night, when the light is poor, more melatonin is produced, making the person sleepy. In the day, it secretes serotonin, making the person active."

"But what does that have to do with dreams?" asked Surya curiously, a tinge of impatience creeping in.

"Later research showed that the pineal gland, although so small and weighing even lesser than previously thought, had a disproportionately high amount of serotonin and was responsible for many functions besides sleep regulation. One of the strangest findings was that the pineal gland could convert serotonin, the happiness hormone, into something far more powerful, into something called DMT."

"What is DMT?" asked Amrit.

"DMT is a chemical secretion that is found in animals and plants. It can also be taken as a hallucinogenic drug, but it is banned in many countries. In fact, even research on it in the USA is classified and needs prior clearance from the Government."

"I yet do not understand how that connects with my dreams," said Surya, even more impatiently.

"Well," said Rajat, gingerly remembering his mentor's advice on how to give bad news to the patient in a gentle manner, "in your dream, you saw Shiva speaking to you, right?"

"Well, not Shiva directly," said Surya, "but I did see a Shivling and I got a message independently."

"Well," said Rajat again, losing all attempts to be tactful, "in the scientific world, it will be termed as a hallucination. Twenty-five grams of DMT secreted by the pineal gland is sufficient for you to imagine statues speaking to you or sending you messages."

Surya looked dazed but Amrit spoke up. "But, doctor, how many grams does the pineal gland produce? You said it was smaller than a pea and yet it manufactures so much DMT?"

"That is the lacuna that science is not able to bridge," said Rajat brightly; he was not trying to make a point against dreams, he was on the side of imparting correct information and he conceded to Amrit's point. "Scientists," he said, "are unable to understand how the pineal gland can produce twenty-five grams of DMT so they are doing research on it. It is too much a quantity for a gland of that size."

Amrit then asked a related question that he was curious about, "Doc, if a person wants to increase the DMT production in his body, then is there something one can do to elevate these levels without external drugs?"

"Research has shown that yoga and meditation substantially affect the secretion of DMT and it can be traced in the blood and organs too. Besides these methods, there are plants that have a high level of DMT that can be ingested. And you need good sleep and food that is free from chemicals. Sugar is particularly bad for it is an inhibitor to the secretion. Therefore, it is possible that the yogis who practice so much yoga and meditation are actually hallucinating due to a higher level of DMT in their bodies."

Surya then spoke, "Doctor, I don't do yoga or meditate and neither is my lifestyle free of sugar so I doubt that I have high DMT levels. However, I have another point; you spoke of the dream as a hallucination but in fact, it was a dream. Does the pineal gland, my third eye, control dreams too?"

"Dream activity is mapped in many different parts of the brain especially the amygdala," said Rajat touching his head to show the location, "but from your description, I would say you believed you had a vision, you acted on it and it is in my opinion, a hallucination."

Amrit wanted to speak up about his telepathic moments but he was not sure. Hesitatingly, he said, "I have not had visions or hallucinations but I did have a very strange telepathic experience." He went on to narrate the strange case of how he had thrown the number '43' to his friend when Rajat intervened, "That is no strange phenomena but a happy coincidence. There are many explanations to it, but loosely, it is the infinity monkey theorem."

"And what is this theorem?" asked Amrit, more than puzzled, his interest piqued.

"Well," said Rajat smiling, "if you give infinite monkeys typewriters or computers these days, then, in a million or infinite tries, one of them will come up with a Shakespearean play."

"I did not understand the connection to my telepathy," said Amrit, bristling a little.

"Your guess of number '43' is one of those coincidences that happen once in a few thousand or million tries. It is not telepathy, just a function of an occurrence of a random sequence."

Amrit wanted to refute the doctor but kept quiet, deciding it was no use speaking to him about how his mother said *'Runtuntun'* when she lay dying in his arms, the voice he had heard when he cremated his mother and about Penaz, the animal communicator, his yoga Masterji who said communication was possible as we were all part of one being.

Rajat continued, inoffensively, even a bit apologetically, "All numbers too are not equal. So, the chance in your case of a number from one to hundred is not really one percent. For example, the person would not think of a single number or a thirteen when asked for a two-digit number. Besides, studies have shown that people tend to choose two numbers with one number adjacent such as 78 or 56 or 43 or 34 or 23."

Amrit murmured, "The person did not choose the number. It was I who threw a selected number in that person's brain," but he realized it was futile and decided to drop the topic.

At this point, the boatman asked Prabod what the doctor was explaining. On getting a gist he said, "The sadhus and saints here have reached enlightenment through their practices. Scientists from Amreeka have tried to explain but your science is no match for the wonders of Mahadev."

Prabod pulled out a flask and some little earthen cups. He poured a little chai for everyone and served it around.

"It's so peaceful here," said Rajat. "Just a kilometer down the Ganga and it is quiet. The city is really very chaotic."

"I was told that sometimes you can see dead bodies afloat on the Ganga," he said, looking at Prabod, his tone more of a question than a statement.

Prabod was unfazed; this was a question he was often asked by tourists. "People do not throw bodies in the Ganga," he said calmly, "and it is illegal too. However, you are right, sometimes one spots a dead body floating in the river. Usually, it is a dead cow or dog but occasionally it is human. That is because everyone is not allowed to be cremated in Varanasi."

All three visitors turned toward Prabod.

"You mean everyone is not equal in cremation? What kind of injustice is this?" asked Amrit.

"It is not injustice," said Rajbir from the end of the boat where he sat. "All people are not equal; some are holier and do not need cremation. It is practical and just."

Surya, Rajat and Amrit looked at him, questioningly and Rajbir continued, "The ones denied cremation are too holy; for example, pregnant women and young children. They cannot be cremated."

"The sadhus too," added Prabod, "are not on the funeral pyre for the same reason."

"Then, there are lepers who are not allowed cremation for the practical reason that their disease is contagious and no one wants to handle their bodies. It is not safe to incinerate them," said Rajbir, "and finally are the special people who have died due to a bite of the cobra."

"Why are they not cremated?" asked Rajat, "Surely a snake bite is not contagious as leprosy is!"

"It is not because of contagiousness," said Rajbir sagely, "a person bitten by a cobra has already been blessed by Shiva and no longer needs further cleansing."

Prabod added an explanation, "The cobra is Shiva's emissary and death by a cobra bite is a form of blessing by Mahadev himself."

"So, what happens to their bodies?" asked Surya who had been unusually silent till now. *My baby was never cremated,* he thought quietly.

"They are supposed to be buried," said Prabod gingerly but Rajbir was less diplomatic.

"Tell them the truth," he said, "stones are tied to their bodies to weigh them and they are thrown into the river. Sometimes the body breaks free and surfaces up. You can occasionally see one in the sunrise cruise."

Amrit shuddered and asked for another cup of the delicious chai.

Rajbir saw his ashen look and said, "You should not let it bother you, sir. What is the body after life has left it? What does it matter to the body how it is disposed of? It is a liability that needs to be got rid of as quickly as possible."

Prabod asked them all to sit. "We will be turning and going toward the main ghats now, so it is better to be seated."

As they approached the ghats, they saw the painted walls appear. There was an abstract modern art across forty feet and next to that was a small painting of a Goddess followed by a giant, multicolored image of Shiva, the deity of the city. Surya spotted a painting on the wall of a lady seated with a saintly halo around her head and on her lap laid the sleeping body of a man.

"Is that the Madonna?" he asked Prabod.

Prabod smiled, "No, sir, that is Mother Savitri."

"I remember reading the story of Savitri in my childhood," said Amrit excitedly, "although I cannot remember it. Please can you give me the gist?"

Prabod cleared his throat and said, "I will tell you the story in a nutshell. Once upon a time, there was a beautiful princess called Savitri. She was very intelligent, well versed in the scriptures and conducted herself excellently."

He looked at Surya smiling and said, "Her father had begotten her through a boon from Surya, the Sun God, after a lot of prayers and Savitri was known for her purity.

The king knew it would be difficult for him to find a suitable husband for Savitri, one who would be as educated as she was, so he asked her to choose her own husband. One day, while on a pilgrimage, she met

Satyavan, a young man who lived in the forest with his parents, an exiled king, who was blind and his queen.

When she returned to her kingdom, she went up to her father who was sitting with Naradji."

"Naradji," intervened Rajbir, "Naradji always comes to add *mirchi* and masala."

Prabod laughed and said, "It's not like that; Naradji is like a facilitator. He carries news from one place to another. In this case, Naradji said that Satyavan was an extremely bad choice as a husband for Savitri because he was not destined to live long. Satyavan would die soon, he said, in fact that he would die in exactly a year from that day. Although her father protested, Savitri was adamant that she would marry Satyavan, notwithstanding the deadly prophecy. So, she was soon married to him, the son of an exiled, blind king, who was destined to die in a year and thus went to live in a hermitage in the forest with him and his family, devoid of material pleasures, dressed as a simple forest dweller.

Weeks and months passed by and Savitri knew it would soon be time before Yama came calling for her husband."

Prabod stopped his narration here as he saw Surya's troubled face. "Are you okay, sir?" he asked Surya. Mukul, the hotel manager had explained to the full team that Surya was an important guest for the hotel and could result in a business tie-up for the future and to take special care of him.

Surya shook his head but Prabod persisted, "If you are feeling seasick, we can stop the tour. I also have a tablet for motion sickness," he said opening a small medicine kit.

"That is not necessary. I was just taken aback when you mentioned Yama. He seems to be coming up a lot these days."

Before Prabod could reply, Rajbir drawled from his side of the boat, "Sir, this is Kashi. You do not have to worry about meeting Yama here; no beginnings here and certainly no endings either. You will only see gulleys, doorways and transformation over here, sir, only transformation."

Surya stared at Rajbir and turned to Prabod. "Please continue with the story."

"Three days before the predicted death date of Satyavan, Mother Savitri started to fast and prayer." All the three visitors noticed how he had added the word Mother to Savitri and how reverential his tone had become. "She would not sleep, but just sit deeply in prayer and meditation. On the appointed day, she approached her blind father-in-law and asked if she could accompany her husband to the jungle.

'Why would you want to go?' he asked Savitri gently. 'It is hot and unsafe; the paths are narrow and full of brambles.'

'It is nearly a year since my marriage,' said the pious Savitri. 'I would like to be with my husband today.'

'You have never asked us for anything in the one year that you have been with us,' said the old king, 'How can I refuse you this small request? But I urge you to be careful, for the jungle is not a safe place.'

Thus, Mother Savitri went into the forest with her husband, quietly chanting her prayers as she walked behind him. Around midday, as Satyavan was chopping a tree for wood, he let out a cry. Mother Savitri ran toward him, her face composed. The time had come, her test had begun. She led Satyavan into a clearing and he lay on the grassy knoll, his head in her lap. 'I feel weak Savitri,' said Satyavan. 'I feel drained of all energy. Something is wrong.'

Mother Savitri stroked his forehead and said, 'Do not worry. I am here. You take a nap; the short rest will do you good.' While Satyavan slept, she started her prayers and vigil.

At first, Yama sent his assistants for Satyavan's *atma* but they could not approach him as he lay on Mother Savitri's lap. When they returned empty-handed, their master asked them where the atma was. 'It is being guarded by one who is too holy,' they reported, 'and we cannot venture near her.' So, Yama decided to go himself to collect the atma of Satyavan. When he reached the forest, the trees had started to cast longer shadows, creating a checkered pattern of light and dark spots. In the middle of a clearing, he saw Satyavan lying, his head resting on the lap of a holy woman and he now understood what his assistants had described. Unhesitatingly, he went and took what he had come for, the atma of Satyavan. Savitri sat in meditation and realized that it was time. She felt the breath of her husband turn still and she knew Yama had come. She opened her eyes and saw the Lord of Death leave with what she wanted to preserve and so, she rose and started to follow him.

Yama heard the tinkling of anklets and turned and saw the holy Mother Savitri following him. 'Go back,' he said gently to her, 'for you cannot come with me. It is not time yet.'

As he turned to proceed, he heard the sound of ankle bells again and turned around once more. 'Go back,' he implored the pious lady, 'you should not be here.'"

"Was she not afraid," asked Amrit, "for Yama is big and dark and fearful, isn't he?"

Again, Rajbir spoke before Prabod could answer, "In the Vedas, Yama is fair and is a king. It is our fear of death, that we associate him to fearful. Here, in Kashi, there is no need to be afraid of Yama, for he is like you and me."

Prabod gave him a wilting look and continued, "Mother Savitri was unafraid. She bent her head with respect and praised the Lord of Death."

"I would have thought she would have asked for Satyavan's life back," said Rajat.

"Ordinary men like us would do that," said Rajbir, "But she is Mother Savitri. She is the epitome of an ideal woman. She wins over the God of Death for her husband's sake."

"To start with, she praised *Dharma*, and how it was necessary to keep the world in balance," said Prabod, "then, she praised Yama as the king of Dharma and finally she correlated the two and praised the Lord of Death, the keeper of Dharma for his fairness and justice, adding words like impartial and keeper of the balance."

"Is Yama known for Dharma?" asked Amrit incredulously. "I have been reading the *Bhagavad Gita* where Dharma is discussed, but I never connected it with Yama."

"Oh yes," said Rajbir, "Yama is called Dharamraj, for it is he who maintains the order in our world, it is he who maintains balance. He is known to be the wisest of the Devatas and he is known to be impartial and fair."

"While it makes so much sense that the Deva in charge of death is the one who is the king of Dharma, I never saw it this way before," said Amrit.

"Please tell us what happened to Savitri," said Rajat.

"You mean Mother Savitri," said Prabod, gently correcting him. "Yamraj was so pleased with the wise words of Mother Savitri, that he offered her three boons. 'Ask me anything,' he said, 'except the life of your husband.'

Without hesitating, Mother Savitri asked that her father-in-law should get back his eyesight and his kingdom too. Yama was impressed that her first wish was not for herself but for her in-laws. 'May it be so,' said Yama gently, tightening his hold on Satyavan's soul.

'My second wish is that my father should have a hundred sons so he has an heir to his throne and he has the comforts of old age.' Yama smiled. He secretly blessed the pious lady in front of him and repeated, 'May it be so.'

Her third wish was for a hundred sons for herself and Yama stretched his hands out and blessed her. 'Finally, you have asked me for something for yourself. So be it, my child,' he said, knowing that he was stepping into a trap for do not forget he is the wisest of the wise, the keeper of Dharma.

'I will need my husband for my children, for my third wish to come true,' said Mother Savitri gently, her head bowed, receiving the blessings from the Deva, 'for I am a pious woman and can have it no other way.'

Yama tried to reason with her but it was already pre-determined. While we think of Yama as fearful, he is kind when needed, and he gently released the atma of Satyavan. 'Go back my child,' he said softly to Mother Savitri, 'for your husband will soon wake up from his sleep. Then, go to your hermitage for your father-in-law has got back his vision and soon he will get his kingdom back too.'

Mother Savitri put her hands together and bowed down. 'We will meet again,' whispered the Lord, 'when the time is right and I will come for you myself then.'"

Prabod ended his story and looked around. The trio was mesmerized. It was the cool weather, the peaceful flowing of the Ganges, the gentle rocking of the boat and the magic of the story that had captivated each one.

Rajat said smilingly, "The story reminded me of my wife. I could see her fighting for my life with Yama."

"It is funny you say that," said Prabod, charmed by the statement, "for this story is narrated to Yuddhisthir in the *Mahabharata* when he claimed that Draupadi surely was the most devoted wife that has existed. He was given the story of Mother Savitri to show that there was one, more devoted, more pious than Draupadi."

*****

Prabod offered them bottles of water and pointed out to the burning ghat again. "We are crossing Manikarnika again," he said. "You are visiting it tomorrow so you will see it up close. But look on the other side. You see the plain sands and empty banks yonder."

They turned to see the other bank of the Ganga, uninhabited and plain.

"Who are those people who are sitting there?" asked Rajat.

Surya and Amrit looked closely and in a distance, they could see small shelters made of bamboo and dried leaves arranged like umbrellas. A few of them were empty but most of the others had a person sitting below, either on a mat on the floor or on a chair.

"What is that there?" asked Rajat again.

"That is called the 'Region of Remorse'," explained Prabod.

"Is it a meditation center? Why is it associated with remorse?"

"After they cremate their loved ones, there are some people who do not come to terms with death. They are filled with sorrow, so they come here and contemplate."

Contemplate, thought Amrit, *what a powerful word. I needed to have come here.* All three of them stared at the people sitting under the umbrellas, in thought. A wind blew and Amrit found himself shivering. Did he just hear the word *Varanasi* whispered in the wind? He looked around sharply to see if the others had heard it too but no one seemed to be reacting. He reeled back a bit and Prabod continued, "They have not found closure, nor have said the things that should have been said when the person was alive. They are full of regret and in some ways, rife with a repentance that has never been expressed."

Amrit could not hear Prabod's words. *Varanasi* the winds seem to chant, echoing the voice he had heard when he had cremated Aai. He always thought it was connected to her death but now as he stared at the mourners, sitting in remorse, he realized with a shock that he knew the voice.

"It is also called a place of penitence. People sit across the river in ruefulness, facing the ghat of cremations. They sit facing the fires and pour out their feelings, draining their bodies of thoughts and words that should have been said earlier."

"And what do they achieve?" asked Amrit softly, his eyes downcast.

"Maybe closure," said Prabod.

Amrit stared at the people sitting there on the banks and wished that he could've been one of them. *Varanasi*, the winds chanted again. In his mind, he replayed the voice that he had heard. It was not Aai; it was Baba who had sent him the message then and it was Baba who was chanting *Varanasi* in his ears through the wind; he had never reached closure with his father's death and that is what had led him here.

He felt his eyes well up and he walked to the other side of the little boat and wiped them with his wrist, hoping nobody would notice them. But Rajbir asked loudly, "Sir, would you want me to take you there? We can go tomorrow." Amrit looked up at him and shook his head. He did not want to answer immediately; he was sure there would be a quiver in his reply and he did not want the others to know that he was emotionally overwrought.

Finally, he asked, his voice husky, "Is it always the son who cremates the parent?"

Prabod said, "Amritji, it is the eldest son who lights his father's funeral."

Amrit asked, "What about the mother?"

"It is the youngest son, in that case," replied Prabod.

"And if the eldest son is not available, in case he is abroad or cannot make it, who then lights the fire?" asked Rajat.

"There is an order," said Prabod, "It's first the eldest son. If he is not there, then the youngest one. And let us assume that he is unavailable as well, then the cremation is performed by any other son. If no son is present, then the son-in-law cremates the body and if he too is absent, then any other male relative."

"What if a man does not have a child?" asked Surya darkly.

"Or if one is not married?" asked Amrit.

"Or if one does not have a son?" asked Rajat.

Prabod looked surprised at the volley of questions but patiently said, "First, the younger brother is the one who performs the rites, else the father or the older brother, and finally, any other relative. It follows that order but in reality, people are no longer too rigid. In fact, nowadays, in a few cases, daughters have started performing the last rites too. Traditionally, only the male members were allowed in the cremation grounds although the scriptures have never forbidden a woman from conducting the rituals."

Surya looked at the mourners sitting in the Region of Remorse and wondered if Jaideep's sons would be sitting here sometime and then shook his head to himself, *I do not understand the dynamics between a father and his children because I don't have any. Who am I to judge who will repent and who will not, who is wronged and who is victimized?* He decided that rather than think of Jaideep and others, he should ensure that he did not feel remorse; he sighed; *I must spend more time with my parents when I get back.*

Rajat then spoke up, "This reminds me of an incident in medical school. We had a few sessions on ethics in the medical world and the lectures were given by a German doctor, a visiting faculty. He was an elderly gentleman and he narrated a small incident, which he said was true, and he used it as a case study. 'There were five friends in college,' said the professor to us, 'who were very close to each other. They spent a lot of time together at the university and stood by each other in laughter and sadness. They traveled and trekked across Germany and as time went by, considered each other as brothers. One night, when it was time to leave university, they sat in a tavern, knowing that life will take them down different paths. One of them said, *We may not be in constant touch as we have been these last few years but know this, that I will carry you all in my hearts wherever I am.* They drank to this and one of them said, *Together, always, in happiness and in sadness.* A third one added, *We are brothers and we will always be there for each other when the other one needs us.* To this a fourth one chimed, *Especially when one of us needs our help, to live or to die.* That night, they made a solid pact between themselves that if any one of them needs the others, then they all must act, even if it was to help one of them to die if that is what he wished for. Years went by and the young men grew up, some married, some had kids, some divorced; they lived in separate cities but remained in touch with each other. When they were in their early seventies, one of the friends was in a coma, and the other four came to visit him. They met his daughter, a middle-aged lady who wept on seeing her father's friends. *The doctor gives us no hope,* she said sadly. *Must he lie as a vegetable then, for the rest of his days?* they asked. *Yes,* she replied, *for his brain is dead.* That night the four somberly sat in a little bar, near their hotel, and raised a toast, *Together, always in life and death.'"*

Rajat paused for a moment like Dr Mehrotra had taught them all, for theatrical effect, and continued, "'the following month, they got the medicine that would release him; they visited the hospital where his still body lay, attached to machines. They hovered around his inert body to block the cameras from picking up any clue and one of them quietly administered the deadly injection to help their brother go to sleep.'"

Rajat then made an unnecessary clumsy turn, an act of flourish that his professor often did, but with more grace than Rajat could ever hope, and said, "Should one play the role of Yama? Was that ethical, to kill a friend? Is it ethical to put a parent to sleep if they are terminally ill or would like to die? What about a pet dog or cat? Will there be remorse? Or relief? Or guilt?"

Surya and Amrit kept quiet but Prabod spoke up. "Sir," he said, "we can never hope to be Yamraj. All of us die when our time comes."

"Do they cremate bodies in Germany?" asked Rajbir.

"Some people do," said Rajat "but more people are buried there."

"Who is it that handles the burning? Is it controlled by the Government?" asked Surya

"It is the Dom Raja who controls all the burning in Kashi. This stretch of land is controlled by him," said Prabod.

"Is this Raja the king of Varanasi?" asked Rajat innocently.

Rajbir broke into peaks of laughter, his belly moving in tandem, "Yes," he said, "he is the Raja of Varanasi and that is his palace," pointing at a three-storied green building with two small, stone lions on the terrace.

Prabod shot him an angry look and looked placatingly at Surya. He hoped that the VIP guest of the hotel did not take offense and he quickly explained. "He is not the erstwhile Raja of Varanasi. The Dom Raja is the person in charge of the cremations, the boss of the people handling the pyres and the lowest of the low, untouchables. It is a job that no one would want."

"But then why does he do it?" asked Amrit, "What is in it for him?"

"A fee must be paid if you want to be cremated in Kashi," said Prabod, "and that money goes to the Dom Raja."

"He must be very wealthy," said Rajat.

"Oh, he is," said Prabod.

"But no one will touch him," said Rajbir, "he is an outcast in society."

"Why is that?" Asked Amrit

"For he is Yama on Earth. The story goes that that eons ago, a golden earring of Mother Parvati fell on this Earth and landed in Varanasi. A Brahmin found it and kept it. When Shivji came for it, he was enraged to see the Brahmin hiding it. 'You shall pay for it,' he said. 'From now on, no one will even touch you. You and your descendants will be the lowest community here.' The Brahmin begged forgiveness, claiming he had intended to return it. You know how soft the heart of Mahadev is. He relented and said, 'You can mind the Eternal Fire and the burning ghat and be useful to the community and earn a living through it.'"

"Is it true that the Dom Raja is Yama on Earth?" asked Surya.

At nearly the same time, Rajat said, "People are shifting to electric crematoriums. Don't they use one in Varanasi?"

Prabod spoke genially. "I will answer both the questions as soon as we approach the next ghat."

The boat moved slowly against the water current and Prabod poured another cup of chai and opened a snack box for the three guests.

Prabod offered a cup to Rajbir too and asked him to stall the boat while the guests sip their tea.

*****

"The ghat you see over there, is the Harishchandra Ghat," he said pointing to a spot, "and that will answer both your questions. This is a cremation ghat too, also very old. The Government has installed an electric crematorium here so that answers your question," he said, turning to Rajat.

"And with regards to your question, sir, there is a story behind Harishchandra Ghat, and with your permission, I can narrate it to you as you all have your chai."

The three men came close together. The weather became cooler and the warm chai tasted more delicious.

Amrit and Rajat sighed with relief when Surya nodded and said, "It will be a pleasure. Please go ahead," as they both wanted to hear the tale.

Amrit would keep finding his eyes darting towards Surya in spite of trying not to. The hair peeping out of the open buttons at the neck mesmerized him. Surya had realized it but ignored it; he was used to the attention from others and had learned not to let it interfere with his interactions.

"Long ago, there was an argument between two sages," said Prabod.

"If you start so far back, the story will be too long and we will never end our tour," said Rajbir.

"You are right," said Prabod. "Let me go ahead in the story else we will never end. Let me start again.

There was a wise king called Harishchandra who, because of some incidents, had decided never to lie and to always walk on the path of truth. He had a beautiful wife and a young son and was loved by his subjects."

"Was he a king from Varanasi?"

"He was the king of Ayodhya, I think," said Prabod making a mental note to recheck his facts, "for he was a descendant of the same dynasty as Lord Ram.

Sage Vishwamitra wanted to test the good king; he had been told that Harishchandra was the most honest and truthful of all men and the sage was sure he could get the king to lose his path of Dharma.

The king was advised to do a big *yagna*, a ritualistic sacrifice to the gods. Vishwamitraji was the presiding priest and after the puja was completed and all the priests were given their due, he stood in front of the noble king and said, 'What about my *Guru dakshina*?'"

"What is a Guru dakshina?" asked Surya.

"It is a fee in the form of a gift or a promise or any form of respect as a token of appreciation that is given, either to a Guru who teaches you or to a spiritual guide who helps you conduct a prayer or ritual like this yagna."

"What did Vishwamitra ask for?" asked Amrit.

"He asked the good King Harishchandra for the kingdom and every material thing he had."

"Was that not too much and out of line with the service he had provided?" asked Rajat.

Prabod was happy to see that all were engrossed in the story. He continued, "This was a test by the sage. In reality, it was too much but Vishwamitraji wanted the honest king to go back on his word.

But Harishchandra did not. He actually gave Sage Vishwamitra his kingdom and left with his wife and little son."

"I think it's a bit harsh, isn't it?" asked Amrit. "I do not see how this sage could qualify to be so learned and do such horrible tests."

Rajbir grinned from one end. "It will become more horrible, sir. Just you wait."

"At the gate of the city, as he was about to leave, the king was stopped. In front of him and his family, stood Vishwamitraji. The king bowed humbly in front of the learned man and Vishwamitraji said, 'You have forgotten one thing.'

Seeing the king look puzzled, he continued, 'You have given me the dakshina but what about the actual fees for the yagna?'

The king was dumbfounded; his queen looked at her husband helplessly but the sage continued his demand, a further test.

'I have nothing,' said the king humbly, 'but give me a month and I will collect the amount for the fees that I owe you.'

King Harishchandra decided to come to Kashi with his wife and little son. By the time they reached the entrance doors to our city, he found the sage standing there.

"Wait a minute," said Rajat, "What do you mean entrance gates to the city?"

"In earlier days, the cities were walled with selected entrances. Timings to enter the city were monitored and the gates were guarded."

"You were saying, when King Harishchandra reached the gates, he found the sage waiting. Please continue, what did the sage want now?"

Prabod grimaced at the bitterness of the tale, "Vishwamitraji informed the king that thirty days were over. His journey and wanderings to Kashi had taken a month and the fees were due on that day.

'But I have just reached and do not have anything yet,' said the king.

A promise is a promise, reminded Sage Vishwamitra hoping that the helpless king would go back on his word. King Harishchandra was taken aback with the attitude of the Sage, but he said forlornly, 'It is yet morning. The day is not over. Meet me tonight and I will have the fees waiting for you.'

The king and his family entered our city of Kashi, hopelessly, for they knew they could never get the fees that they needed to give the sage by night time. 'What will we do?' asked the good queen, 'Maybe we should kill ourselves?'

'I would gladly give up my life,' said Harishchandra blankly, 'but my debt to Sage Vishwamitra will not be repaid and I will die in dishonor owing somebody money. I cannot do that, nor can I carry forward this debt to my next life.'

By afternoon, they were demoralized and dejected. In despair, the queen made another suggestion. 'Sell me as a slave,' she said 'and make good our debt with the money you get.' 'How can I sell my wife?' said the king and the two of them wept, disconsolate for they knew it was the only option if the king wished to save his honor. King Harishchandra stood in the market and offered his wife; people gathered and mocked the man who would sell his wife, but an elderly man stepped forward and paid the asking price. As the queen was about to leave with the buyer, her young son started wailing. 'He wants his mother,' said the king to the buyer of his wife. The queen stood still, also weeping silently for her son, for the turn of fate and for the separation from her husband. 'Good sire,' said Harishchandra to the elderly man who had bought the queen, 'can you also buy the little boy so he can be with his mother?' The old man nodded; money was exchanged and the little prince was sent along with his mother to serve in the house of the elderly man.

King Harishchandra sought out Vishwamitra and gave him the money he had got from selling his wife and son. 'Here are your fees,' he said, 'now set me free.' The sage counted the money and shook his head, 'We are yet short of a small amount,' he said, hoping the king would now give up.

'I have hardly an hour left,' said the desperate king looking at the setting sun's position in the sky, 'I will sell myself.' He went back to the market, this time to sell himself, but it was getting dark and there were few people there. 'Who will buy me?' said the king in the marketplace and people scoffed at him. 'Isn't he the man who sold his own wife and son earlier today?' they jeered. 'He is so weak. Who will want to buy him?' mocked another person. However, a shriveled man, dark, scarred and bent came forward and said, 'I will buy you sire and you will have to do my bidding.'

With no option, King Harishchandra sold himself to the buyer, who was the man who cremated the dead on the ghats of the river, at this very spot. The king gave the money he had gotten to the sage to complete the fees demanded and meekly followed his new master."

"Is this why this ghat is called the Harishchandra Ghat?" asked Rajat.

"The story is yet not over, Sir," said Rajbir, "The worst has yet to come."

Prabod swallowed and continued, "Months passed by and Harishchandra was now in charge of the cremation grounds. He would take fees from the people who came to cremate their loved ones and he would prepare the pyres and handle the corpses. His face grew dark and stained with the fires he tended, his hands charred and scarred. Very often, he wondered what had led him to this misfortune. One night, when he lay in his hut, he heard a voice. It was a lady, a maid, dressed in a white garment, carrying the corpse of a child. 'I need to cremate my son,' she said, her voice devoid of emotion, her face deadened. King Harishchandra stared at the woman and recognized her as his wife; he realized that she did not know who he was. His heart broke to see his son dead, in the arms of his wife, a slave girl now."

At this point, Prabod's voice began to quiver a little and he continued, "King Harishchandra asked the queen for the fees to cremate their child. 'I am afraid I do not have anything,' she said softly. 'But I cannot continue without the fees,' he lamented ruefully, 'for my master has imposed that rule for all people who wish to use our facilities.'"

A tear escaped from Prabod's eyes and Rajbir continued the story, "Prabodji, why don't you take a break and let me continue the story. You can have a cup of chai; else it will be too cold to drink."

Rajbir turned to the three listeners and said, "The queen tore half of her garment that covered her modesty and gave it to the keeper of fires, her husband, as the fees to cremate their son. King Harishchandra could contain himself no more and he revealed his identity to his wife and they both clung on to each other, weeping for their son and their misfortune. 'Let us now jump into the fire along with our son,' said the queen and the king agreed.

At that point, the master of the cremation ground came, the wizened shriveled man, and said, 'Stop King Harishchandra for it was only a test.' The master was none other than Yama, and he is the originator of the lineage of Dom Rajas, the keepers of the cremation grounds. Sage Vishwamitra too appeared and conceded defeat in his test of the honesty of the king. The elderly man who had bought the queen and the prince was none other than Indraji, Lord of the Devas. They said it was a mirage and the prince is alive and the kingdom of Harishchandra was untouched where the king and queen would return."

Prabod then spoke up, recovered, a little awkward and embarrassed, "This ghat is the cremation ground where the noble and truthful King Harishchandra worked in our city and we have named the spot after him."

Surya looked at Prabod and said, "You eventually mention Yama in every story? You say this city belongs to Shiva but all your tales deal with Yama."

Prabod smiled. "Shiva is everywhere," he said cryptically, "even when he is not mentioned in a story."

But Surya persisted, "Do you know of anyone who has met Yama and lived to tell the tale?"

"Ha-ha," laughed Rajbir loudly, his belly vibrating. "You are lucky if you meet Yama here in Kashi," he said, "for then moksh is guaranteed. Tell him about Nachiket, the boy who visited Yama," said Rajbir from his end of the boat.

"We have no time for more stories," said Prabod, "for we will soon reach the hotel. In fact, I need to call the receptionist and inform them that Suryaji will be back soon."

It was already dark as they were approaching the hotel and they were looking forward to getting back. It had been a long day for Surya and Amrit who had traveled that morning itself.

As they sailed past, Surya spotted a painting on a wall, it was of a Shivling and he felt a shiver down his spine. It was not the one in his dream but it reminded him eerily of it. The image highlighted the real reason for his trip to Varanasi; it was not really for a business tie-up with Kailash Kothi but to find the idol of his dreams that had sent him the messages. Tomorrow he would be in the most important Shiva temple in Varanasi and he would finally have met the messenger who visited him in his sleep.

Prabod noticed Surya staring at the painting and said gently, "In Kashi, we worship Shivji as a householder and also as a *vairagya.*"

"Who is a vairagya?" asked Surya.

"A person who has developed inner spirituality so has chosen to give up everything external," said Prabod. "You can call him a renunciate who has discovered the path to moksh."

"So Shivji gives up his family?" asked Rajat.

"No," said Prabod, "Shivji was detached and a renunciate after the death of his first wife. It took a lot of penance from Mother Parvati to make him break his resolve and start life again as a householder."

"It is symbolic," said Rajbir. "You can find your moksh as a householder or as a detached renunciate, the choice is always yours. There is one destination but many paths leading there."

"Having said that, we have reached Kailash Kothi, which is our destination," said Prabod smiling.

Mukul was waiting for the guests; he singled Surya and said, "Did you have a good time?"

Surya nodded and said, "It was truly enlightening. Your team here is very knowledgeable."

Mukul beamed, "Come, sir, we have a special dinner waiting for you," and led Surya away into the hotel.

CHAPTER 5

VARANASI, DAY TWO, MORNING

"Everything will be okay in the end…. if it's not okay, it's not the end."

It was five in the morning; the alarm rang and Amrit woke up with a start. He looked around, wondering for a moment where he was; he sighed and closed his eyes again. He was in the midst of such a good dream and he wanted to go back under the comforting sheets but he shook himself up for it was an important day for him. He looked outside from the little window and saw it was yet dark. He wondered why the receptionist at the hotel had asked him to leave so early in the morning to put Aai's ashes in the river; it is auspicious to put it at sunrise he had said and Amrit had quietly agreed.

Amrit stepped down to the hotel lobby, holding the precious container. He was glad that he had booked a private boat to take him to submerge Aai's ashes. His mother would have been shocked to know he was spending so much for the task and would have undoubtedly dissuaded him, asking him to submerge the ashes in the sea near their house. He himself had been reluctant when he had checked the prices but Gagan had solemnly told him that he had to hire a private boat and Amrit had overcome his sensibilities and agreed to spend the money.

Amrit stepped out of the hotel into the darkness. The air was cold, a light breeze blew and he shivered involuntarily. It has been nearly a year since Aai passed away he thought. I will place her ashes in the water as I had planned; just a small ride into the waters and back. Sunil, the receptionist, stepped out of the hotel and said, Rajbirji will guide you. You know him already; he was the boatman on yesterday's cruise.

Amrit nodded, unable to speak, surprised at himself for being choked. He had not expected himself to get so emotional. Sunil did not wait for a reply and proceeded, "I have explained your requirements to Rajbirji. He will take you to the right spot in the river."

Amrit nodded and followed Sunil, carefully holding the leak-proof plastic box containing the ashes. *I shouldn't let the box fall into the river when I empty its contents*, he suddenly thought to himself, *Aai was always so possessive of her tiffin boxes; she would never forgive me if I carelessly lost one of them.*

Amrit walked into the boat, gingerly, clasping the box to his chest. Rajbir looked at him but did not smile for he knew that Amrit would be overwrought with emotions. He quietly helped him aboard.

"Can I wear the life jacket?" asked Amrit. The boatman wished to tell him that it was not required but he wordlessly handed him the neon orange jacket and Amrit wore it meticulously. Rajbir started the motor and the sound seemed out of place in the surroundings. The boat started to glide in the dark waters, gentle waves being created, and wordlessly moved away from the hotel. The banks resounded with the early clanging of temple bells, and the ghats already seemed dotted with people saying their morning prayers. The sun had not yet arisen, but pale light broke through the darkness on the horizon, announcing the imminent arrival of daybreak.

They rode in silence for the next few minutes until they reached a more open spot, away from the ghats. Rajbir cut off the motor and said, "We will park here for a little while."

Amrit understood the cue and rose, and quickly held the side of the boat, realizing that his knees were a bit shaky. He looked around, the blackness of the sky yielding to dawn arising from the east, the waters placid and flowing gently and he felt that he was witnessing a sight that was timeless.

"We are in the epicenter of the Universe," said Rajbir in a low voice, "at the point where Creation starts and ends. This is a good spot." So profound was the scene, that for that moment, Amrit believed Rajbir's words to be true. He steadied himself, looked at the boatman and asked, "Should I put the ashes in here?"

"Yes," said Rajbir, "let your mother start her eternal journey. Ganga *Maiya* is patiently waiting so you can take your time."

Amrit clicked the box open and carefully set the lid on the side. He leaned forward and he saw the dark water lapping on the side of the boat. In the dawn light, it seemed dark and mysterious, deep and alluring. He gently turned the plastic container and the ashes poured out. *Goodbye Aai,* he said to himself. *I have much to thank you for; you accepted me for what I was, your love was unconditional and you nurtured and protected me. Farewell Aai.* The river swallowed most of the ashes; a few floated away.

Amrit sighed and turned to seat himself. He was surprised, even a trifle disappointed as to how quickly it had all happened.

He turned to see the waters, wanting to dip his hands in the water and stir it to ensure the ashes had dissolved but he dared not, for fear of falling in; for fear that the river would swallow him as it had his mother's ashes, for fear of the bacteria and pollution that he had heard about in the sacred waters, for fear of accosting a dead body that had broken its shackles and surfaced as had been discussed the day before. He looked at the vast river flowing and it seemed eternal, and he understood why people came here to die.

"Should we go?" asked Rajbir gently.

"I would like to sit here for a few minutes if you do not mind," said Amrit.

"We have plenty of time, sir," said the boatman.

"No, we do not," said Amrit wistfully. "One day we too shall fade away, our lights extinguished, never to return. We do not have a lot of time."

"We all come back except the few," said Rajbir quietly.

The sun rose in the distance and flooded the river with gold. A bird flew by overhead and somewhere a cow lowed.

"Who are the lucky few who do not return?" asked Amrit listlessly

"The ones who have learned what they must learn, the ones blessed with moksh. Unless, of course, you are Markandeya."

"Who is Markandeya? And how did he evade death?"

"I will tell you the story briefly as we sit here. There was a sage called Mrikandu who was childless. His wife and he prayed ceaselessly to Shivji. After several months of prayer, Shivji appeared in a dream and asked Mrikandu whether he would like a hundred sons who would live for a long time but would be foolish or if the sage would like one son who would be extremely wise and intelligent but would live for only sixteen years. Mrikandu chose the latter and soon he was blessed with a son, who he called Markandeya.

As promised, Markandeya was gifted and quickly learned the Vedas and holy books. He was humble and was liked by everyone around him. Years passed and Markandeya would soon be sixteen years, his final year. His parents were inconsolable but Markandeya told them not to worry. I will worship Shivji and He is compassionate. I am sure He will find a way out.

On his sixteenth birthday, Markandeya sat praying to a Shivling when Yama came for him, astride his bull, a lasso in his hand. 'It is time to go,' said Yama to the teenager but Markandeya continued to pray, clasping the Shivling in fervent prayer. Yama got his noose ready and threw it around Markandeya to take him; the noose landed around the boy and the Shivling and Yama started to tighten it. From the Lingam, rose the mighty Mahadev, in anger at being caught in Yama's noose. Yama shrank back in apology and Mahadev asked him to leave without Markandeya and blessed the boy with a long life. Thus, Markandeya was spared from death and went on to become one of our greatest Rishis of all time."

"That was interesting," said Amrit, "but now, let us go back. I am feeling cold here."

"Do you want me to take you to the Region of Remorse, which we spoke about yesterday?"

"No," said Amrit, "I just want to go back and sit in my room alone for some time."

The boatman nodded, started the motor and directed the boat back to Kailash Kothi.

When Amrit's boat approached the jetty of the hotel, he saw Surya standing at the top of the ghat. He was dressed in a pure white kurta and narrow pants looking very appealing; Amrit gulped bewitched, guilty that his base instincts were aroused so soon after the pious and emotionally laden act that he was returning from.

He then noticed that Surya had another man next to him, with whom he was talking animatedly. The companion was a local, decided Amrit, swarthy skin, coarse hair, neatly but unfashionably cut, *at the roadside barbershop*, thought Amrit. Amrit removed his life jacket, jumped off the boat with more confidence than before and thanked Rajbir. He walked up the steps and Surya saw him and waved out.

"I will see you after lunch," called Surya to Amrit and turned to follow the other man.

*****

Surya woke up early, excited that he was finally going to meet the statue of his dreams. "I am finally here," he said to himself, "and I must ask the dark Lord why I have been called." He looked at his mobile phone repeatedly to check the time. He decided to go to the lobby and wait for the guide who would take him to the temple rather than pace in his room.

Sunil, the receptionist, jumped up on his feet when he saw Surya. "Is everything okay, sir? Do you need something?" he asked with genuine concern.

"Nothing," replied Surya expansively, for he was full of excitement, "I am down early, waiting for my guide."

Sunil looked at his notes and saw that he had no information for a guide for the VIP guest. With a worried tone, he asked, "Is there a booking for a guide with us?"

"It has been arranged by my office."

As they were speaking, a man entered the little lobby and asked, "Are you Suryaji?"

Surya looked at smiled at the man, "Are you the guide booked by my office?"

"Yes," said the man, "Tusharji from Mumbai has asked me to show you the Kashi Vishwanath temple this morning."

They stepped out and the guide smiled and said, "I forgot to introduce myself. My name is Dharam." He rolled up his sleeves and Surya smiled as he saw the green tattoo on his hand. It read 'Dharam' in the Devanagari script and there was an outline of a bull's head after the name. Surya noticed that the guide limped as he walked but decided to say nothing of it.

Surya looked at him closely, into his eyes, and smiled warmly. "Let's go," he said animatedly, "I have waited for too long to visit the temple and cannot wait anymore. Is it too early to visit the temple?" He spied Amrit coming up the steps from the ghats and waved out.

Dharam led Surya up the stairs. "Don't worry about my limp. I am comfortable with it. I had an accident on one leg but it does not bother me," said Dharam, when he saw Surya looking at him climbing the steps with a little effort. Dharam continued, "The temple opens at three in the morning," he said. He had been informed that Surya was a special guest and could lead to a lot of business. "I have arranged a special darshan for you."

They took the waiting car toward the temple. Surya had been working in the travel business for the past few years and had traveled a lot within India, meeting many people in different fields of the same business and so he could mentally slot them in his first meeting itself. He found Dharam to be very sure of himself, very collected and confident, his stride was sure in spite of a bad leg, his voice deep and his words crisp. Although Surya would prefer to be quiet and reflective on this temple visit, he asked Dharam a lot of questions, for he needed to see if the guide's knowledge was vast and whether his presentation interesting, in case of a potential future tie-up.

"How old is the temple?" he asked earnestly, "And tell me more about the Shivling."

"There are many stories in Varanasi so I can tell you the facts and the legend. What would you like to hear first?"

Surya was more interested in the legend if anything at that point in time but he knew that as a person in his trade, he had to ask for the facts first. "I would like to hear both. Why don't you start with the facts but keep them brief for I have many questions?"

Dharam smiled and started, "The temple, Kashi Vishwanath, was destroyed and rebuilt several times and is supposed to be very old as it has been mentioned as long back as in the Puranas. About nine hundred years ago, Qutbuddin Aibak demolished the temple but it was rebuilt by Iltutmish."

"So, what we will see is the temple rebuilt by Iltutmish?"

"No," said Dharam, "That temple too was razed by Sikandar Lodhi but then the temple was built again over five hundred years ago in the reign of King Akbar. It was rebuilt by Queen Jodhabai's father, Raja Mansingh; however, the local Hindus did not accept the temple as they felt Raja Mansingh had betrayed the Hindu cause by giving his daughter, Jodha, to the Muslim Mughal king in marriage."

Surya started to speak but stopped as Dharam continued, "But it was finally destroyed when Aurangzeb took over the Mughal throne. The sacred Shivling of the temple itself was thrown in the well nearby and the place was converted into a mosque. The presiding priest of the temple jumped into the well to save the Shivling."

"From what I remember, is it not said that if an idol develops a crack, it can no longer be used?" asked Surya.

"You are right, sir," said Dharam, "When a statue gets a crack, it is believed that the deity, living within, or the sanctity of the statue leaves it and so is not used. Such a statue is left in flowing water to melt away or erode back to the elements. But in this case, the Shivling was intact, saved by the head priest."

"But this is not the original temple?" asked Surya

"It is not," said Dharam and he stared at Surya. Surya looked up for he felt Dharam's look pierce his eyes and enter his body and he felt naked and vulnerable. "About fifty years ago, Rani Ahilyabai Holkar, the great queen of Indore, had a dream. Shivji appeared and asked her to rebuild the temple. Great things are conveyed in dreams," he added slowly.

When he heard Dharam speak about Shiva appearing in the dreams, Surya felt as if a searing rod had passed through his mind and he stared at Dharam.

"Maharana Ranjit contributed the gold for the three domes. It is said that if you look at the domes with faith, you attain moksh, but that is a legend of course."

Surya sat silent and then finally asked, "What is the legend of the temple?"

Dharam smiled and continued, "According to the Skanda Purana, when the first ray of light hit Earth, it is said, that it touched Kashi, our sacred Varanasi. Brahmaji and Vishnuji got into a disagreement on their powers, and Shivji was called to mediate. He created a column of light, the first Shivling, called the Jyotirling, a shaft of brilliant light, at this very spot where the temple stands and then Shivji asked them to locate the source of the light. Brahmaji used the swan, his vehicle, to try and locate the top of the pillar while Vishnu took the form of Varaha, the boar, to locate its bottom but neither could find the start or the finish. The lingam of the temple is a miniature of the original first Jyotirling, the shaft of light that crosses three worlds, from the netherworld, splitting through Earth and piercing the skies, forming a central axis. It is a perfect place to cross over from Earth to the other realm.

Legend has it that true devotees who visit the temple will be released from life by Shivji himself for Yama is not allowed in this temple."

Surya was startled at the mention of the Lord of Death. "Yama crops up again and again in my trip to Varanasi," he said. "Yesterday, when we took the cruise ride, the boatman said there was a boy who met Yama and lived to tell the tale."

Dharma smiled and looked intently at Surya; once again he felt himself getting hypnotized. "Yes, there was a boy called Nachiket. Legend says that the young Nachiket was helping his father, a famous sage, conduct a dakshina yagna, a prayer in which one gives away a lot of one's material possessions. Nachiket noticed that his father was giving away cows that were old and derelict and would not be of use to the receiver, while he kept the healthy ones for himself. The young lad knew that the sacrifice that his father was conducting would be in vain if performed with greed, instead of a true donation, so he interrupted his father to get him to correct his action. His father was busy but the boy kept butting in. Finally, he asked the sage, 'Father, you are giving away all your wealth, so to whom are you giving me, for I too am part of your wealth?'

His father ignored the question, but Nachiket persisted. In a fit of temper, the learned man told his son, 'Nachiket, I have given you to Yama.'

Everyone around was nonplussed at the words and the sage started to apologize to his son but Nachiket smiled and said, 'Do not fret, father, for I will go to meet Yama as you have taught me that we must never go back on our word.' The old man wept and begged but his son was adamant and soon left for Yama's abode."

Surya interrupted the guide here and asked him, "Where does Yama stay? Where did the young Nachiket go?"

Dharam smiled, "People guess that he must have come to the ancient city of Kashi where man meets the Devas but it is never mentioned. The story goes on from the point that Nachiket reached the house of the Lord of Death and waited patiently outside for three days and nights since Yama was not at home. He was offered water and food but he desisted, preferring to wait for the master of the house to return. When Yama came, riding on the back of his bull, he saw a little boy waiting outside his house. Yama went in to freshen up and his family was agog. 'There is a young lad waiting for you for three days,' they said. 'He has not had anything to eat or drink. This is no way to treat a guest; a curse by him could harm us. Please go and mollify him.'

Yama stepped outside to meet the young Nachiket and gently said to him, 'Young boy, you have come from afar. You have waited patiently for me for three days and nights so I will give you three wishes. Ask me for anything and they will be yours.'"

Surya was invested in the story and looked at Dharam eagerly. "What did Nachiket ask for?" he inquired.

"Nachiket's first wish was for his father. 'Please, sir, my father was very upset when I left home. Undoubtedly, he is repentant and inconsolable so please make him happy again and let him know that I am fine. When I go back, let him receive me well.' Yama was surprised at the young lad's first wish and simply said, 'So be it.' Nachiket's second request was a wish that would be for his society in general. He asked Yama to explain the rituals to be conducted at the time of death, for the easy migration of the atma. Yama impressed by the boy's unselfish question, explained the procedures in great detail. However, it was the third wish that bowled over Yama."

"What was the third wish?" asked Surya in anticipation.

"Nachiket wanted to know the story of death. What happens to the soul after a person dies and how can one be immortal? Yama did not know how to evade the question and avoid giving a reply; he hawed and hemmed, he implored the young lad to choose another wish, he tempted Nachiket with immeasurable wealth, of many sons, a prosperous life, beautiful women but Nachiket was adamant. 'All that you offer me is transitory,' he said, 'for one day, I will have to die. In my third wish, I want to know the story of death and moksh.'"

Surya was finding it difficult to breathe. Something in the story had touched him and he felt it connected to his own dream and his state of mind. His voice came out, nearly in a whisper, "What did Yama tell the boy?"

The driver slowed the car and someone crossed their path hurriedly, making the car swerve. "Har Har Mahadev," said the driver and Dharam looked at him and smiled.

"That is what Yama explained to Nachiket," and seeing the puzzled expression on Dharam's face, he explained, "Har Har Mahadev."

"But he must have spoken about the migration of the atma," said Surya.

"Yes, he spoke about the atma, about Brahman and moksh," said Dharam.

"What exactly is moksh?" asked Surya.

"It is a small word but with a big meaning. We have reached the temple so we can discuss it later. We have the afternoon together too."

"I have two friends with me for the afternoon trip. I hope that will not be a problem for you," said Surya.

"You can call the full world and it is not a problem for me, I can manage them all," said Dharam proudly.

They stepped out of the car, and Dharam said, "Normally, we have to go to the temple office ahead to get the entry pass and take a priest to help you see the temple inside. You need to keep all your belongings there in a locker. But we have made special arrangements for you, sir. You can leave your things in the car and I will be waiting here for you."

"Are you not coming inside to show me around?" Surya asked puzzled.

"I am afraid I cannot for guides are not allowed. However, I have arranged for the temple priest to take you in directly, without the lengthy procedures."

Surya felt light-headed; he was here at last; the mystery of his dreams would be solved finally and he was giddy in anticipation. He emptied his pockets and mobile phone in a bag in the car and then remembered the question he had been meaning to ask. "You said that Yama is not allowed in this temple, so then has no one died here?"

"Ha-ha," smiled Dharam, "you pick up a lot of details. Indeed, Yama is not allowed in this temple for it is Shivji who releases the atma of the dead in this temple. Now go sir, for the priest is waiting to take you in."

Dharam introduced Surya to the priest, a short pot-bellied man wearing a cream-colored dhoti. "Please bring sir back to this same spot, show him everything in detail, there is no hurry," he instructed the priest who nodded and led Surya within the temple.

Surya passed through the metal detectors in a trance, waiting to reach the main idol; he hardly heard the history of the temple that the priest kept sonorously narrating.

"Please take me to the Shivling, I need to go there first," said Surya.

They went to the temple within the complex, which was crowded and noisy; the priest accompanying Surya said something loudly to the other priests. They cleared a few people on the side and let Surya come near a silver square basin that housed the Shivling that had been callously thrown in a well several hundred years ago and saved by the head priest. Surya bowed down, a tear rolling from his eye in disappointment, for this was not the statue that had appeared in his dreams. It was unbearable, for he had come all the way to Varanasi with the hope that he will have his dream explained, he was sure and excited but the truth was not here for him and he felt broken, a little cheated and somewhat foolish.

The guiding priest led him away; he was impressed to see the tears from Surya's eyes, mistaking them as a mark of devotion. "This temple does bring out many emotions," he said loudly and a little pompously, his chest swelling as if he was responsible for the greatness of the temple. "It is the seat of spirituality and many saints have been moved as you have been. Tulsidasji wrote the *Ram Charit Manas* in Varanasi and visited the temple often, and so did Adi Shankaracharyaji, who consolidated the Vedas. Guru Nanakji too came here while creating a new religion and so did Satya Sai Baba."

Surya was unable to mouth his misgivings to the rotund priest, nor his disappointment and sorrow. Others may have found solace in this Shivling but he had not found what he was searching for. He remembered the words of the boatman the previous day, *Shivji is not to be found in the temples in Varanasi. He is everywhere.*

Surya turned to the priest and said, "Let us go."

"Before you go, you must whisper in the ears of Nandiji."

"Why would I whisper in Nandi's ears?" asked Surya.

The priest did not answer but led him to the Nandi of the temple. It was impressively large, over seven feet tall.

"Let us sit here, so I can tell you why you should whisper in the ears of Nandiji, the bull."

They sat on the steps nearby and the priest started his story, speaking loudly; Surya looked around but no one seemed disturbed. Surya wanted to tell the priest to lower his volume but he felt too dejected to say anything.

The priest boomed along, "There was a learned man in the past, someone like me you can say," he paused here, his chest puffing a little more, "his name was Shilada. He prayed incessantly to Mahadev and when Shivji appeared in front of him, he bowed down and said, 'Lord, I would like to have a child.'"

Surya listened to the poorly narrated tale listlessly and the priest continued, "The next day, when he was in the fields, he saw an infant lying, a baby boy, shining brighter than the daylight. Shilada took him home, adopted him and gave him the name, Nandi. He showered great love on the child, teaching him the holy scriptures and everything he knew. Nandi was a bright boy and quickly grasped all the teachings. Years passed and the baby grew up to be a young man. One day, two sages came to their little house and Shilada welcomed them; he asked Nandi to take care of the two learned souls. Nandi served the holy men well during their stay and soon it was time for them to leave. Shilada and Nandi prostrated themselves to touch the feet of the sages and asked for their blessings; they first blessed Shilada with a long and prosperous life but when they turned to Nandi, they faltered and stuttered a blessing to be well and listen to his elders. When the sages left, Shilada realized that something was amiss; he ran to meet the two visitors and asked them why they had faltered when they blessed his beloved son. They awkwardly explained to Shilada that his son, Nandi, did not have a long life so they could not bless him with one for he was fated to die young. They gave him the blessings they could think of on the spur of the moment. Shattered by this news, Shilada returned ashen-faced back to his house.

'What is wrong?' asked Nandi and Shilada recounted to him what the wise men had said. He looked at Nandi dolefully but was surprised to his son smiling. 'Is that all, father?' asked the young Nandi, 'Where is your faith in Shivji who is all giving and compassionate? I was born through his wishes and I will live through him too.' The next day, Nandi stood in the river near their house and started his austere penance to Shivji."

The priest turned to Surya and said, "No one gives so much information to visitors. I hope you are happy with all the stories I am telling you."

Surya nodded; he knew the priest was reminding him to give a good tip at the end but he was too dejected to say much. He gently asked, "Did Shivji come?"

The priest beamed, "The Lord is known for his soft heart. He can never ignore the penance of a devotee. He appeared in front of Nandi. The young boy was spellbound; never had he experienced anything so encompassing. Shivji gently asked the boy, 'What would you like?' And the boy instinctively replied, 'To be with you always.' Shivji smiled his mysterious smile and said, 'My bull has recently died and I can use another vehicle. Would you take the head of a bull and be my mount, my guardian, my keeper and watch? You will be with me always.' Nandi bowed down, happy that he was the chosen one."

The priest ended with a flourish, "And that was the story of Nandi."

Surya was unwilling to end the story, his interest piqued. "That does not answer my question. Why should one whisper in Nandi's ears?" he asked wryly

The plump pundit sighed. This customer would take his tip money's worth of information. He wanted to roll his eyes but instead smiled benignly. "I have many other commitments to attend to but I will yet give you this information," he said.

"In a temple, the statue of Nandi always faces his master and Lord, waiting for a command," said the priest.

"Hey wait," said Surya, "in this temple, the Nandi is not facing the Shivling."

"My dear sir," said the priest patronizingly, "Ah, yes, I was about to mention it – the original temple was destroyed and a mosque was built where the earlier temple structure stood. This temple is beside the original structure. The Nandi is yet facing where the idol rested in the original temple."

"Oh yes, I do remember now," said Surya sheepishly.

"Well, once Shivji and Nandi sat in deep meditation at Mount Kailas; at the same time, an evil Asura came to take Shivji's wife, Mother Shakti, away. Everyone knew that Shivji had to be immediately informed about this abduction but were scared to disturb him while he was meditating. They decided to approach his son, Ganeshji, to inform his father that his wife has been carried away. His son, too, was fearful of interrupting his father at this time but it was necessary so he came up with a plan. He whispered in Nandi's ears and sure enough, the message reached Shivji who came out of his trance to take the necessary action."

The round priest smiled and concluded, "So then, we all knew that by whispering in Nandi's ears, the message goes directly to Shivji. Why don't you whisper in Nandi's ear now and then I will escort you out?"

Surya went closer to the large statue of the bull not knowing what to ask; there was so much to ask and yet nothing seemed to come to his mind at that moment. Should he ask for a child like all the sages in the stories had asked for? Or should he ask for happiness? Or should he be like the boy Nachiket and ask a boon for someone else? He smiled at himself; *so many decisions to whisper in the ear of a stone bull?* He shook his head and told the priest, "I have nothing to ask now. We can leave."

But then he stopped and said, "Wait a minute, I do have something to ask."

He walked respectfully to the large bull statue and put his mouth toward the ear, careful not to touch his lips to the stone and said, "Nandi, take my wish to Shiva and ask him to let me know who is it that comes in my dreams and beckons me to meet him."

Surya sat in the car and put on his sunglasses.

Dharam, the guide, sat in the front seat and turned around and asked, "I hope you had good darshan."

"Yes and no," said Surya. "The priest arranged it well, so yes, I had good darshan. No, because I had dreamed of something and this was not what I expected."

Dharam smiled and said, "You never know where one's dreams may materialize. Maybe we look for them in the wrong places while they are waiting for us elsewhere."

"Let us return to the hotel," said Surya half-heartedly.

Dharam looked at his watch. "We have time," he said, "Can I take you someplace else?"

"I would like to get back to the hotel as I have a lot of paperwork," said Surya. He had to fill in the analysis form that his team had developed to evaluate a new property that they may tie-up with. He had to prepare for the mid-morning meeting with the manager, which would spill into early lunch. There was a lot to be done this morning.

Dharam instructed the driver to take them to the hotel. "We will stop on the way to let Suryaji taste the *malaiyo* of Varanasi," he said

"What is that?" asked Surya.

"It is a local delicacy, a sweetened froth of milk and morning dew. It's available only for a short period, during the winter months. It's very famous here and on the way to the hotel."

At the hotel, Surya bade goodbye to Dharam.

"I will come at 2 p.m. for the afternoon tour of the gulleys and ghats of Varanasi," he said before leaving.

*****

As Surya was collecting his room keys, Rajat emerged from the elevator and walked toward the reception desk.

The doctor was excited and he said to Surya, "I am going to taste the *kachori* breakfast. Would you like to come with me? I have heard it's excellent and not worth missing."

"Thank you," said Surya, "but I have a lot of work to finish this morning. I will not be able to come with you, but let's meet at the lobby at 2 p.m. today for the afternoon tour."

"That's perfect," said Rajat and turned to Prabod the hotel assistant, "Let's go to sample the kachoris."

As Prabod took Rajat through the tiny bylanes of Varanasi to breakfast on the famous delicacy, the good doctor was appalled and at the same time, fascinated by the endless labyrinth of lanes that defied grid lines and mapping. He was a bit unsettled when he saw the stall selling the kachoris but surmised that they would be excellent, judging by the huge crowd of people who had also come for the same purpose.

"Is it safe to eat here?" he asked Prabod for the restaurant (though you could hardly call it that) looked unhygienic. Rajat looked balefully at the little lane, crowded with waif-like stray dogs with hunger written all over their face, their rib cage showing pitifully through their mangy coats.

"Don't worry, sir," assured Prabod, "all the big actors and industrialists from Mumbai visit this place."

Rajat cautiously ordered a plate while Prabod stood respectfully on the side. While Rajat was eating, Prabod gently suggested, "Would you like to buy something for your wife sir?"

"For my wife?" asked Rajat puzzled, his forehead scrunched, for he could not remember having mentioned anything of that sort. He continued to bite into the delicious snack, laden with calories and fat but irresistible as promised.

"During the boat ride yesterday, you mentioned that she loved you a lot and you could imagine her warding off Yama as Mother Savitri had done, so I thought you might want to take something for her from here. We are famous for Benarasi sarees and I am sure she will love it."

Rajat paused to think so Prabod continued, "The shop is very close by too."

"Will it be open so early?" enquired Rajat, with no real intention of buying anything.

"Normally they are shut at this hour, but the owner is known to me, so he will open it especially for you."

When he saw Rajat hesitating, he added, "He will also give a big discount."

"I don't know," said Rajat.

"Sir, why not go and have a look. There is no compulsion to buy. Besides, you are lucky to have such a good wife; I am sure that you will want to buy her something special."

And thus, Rajat went along with Prabod to buy a gift for his wife; a saree in purple and yellow, which his wife would never wear.

On the way to the shop, Prabod said, "Like the story of Mother Savitri, there is another story of the son of King Hima; let me narrate it to you as we walk to the silk shop and it will also remind you of how lucky you are to have a devoted wife.

There was a famous king called Hima; he had a son, whom he loved a lot. It had been predicted that this boy would die of a snake bite on his sixteenth birthday and the king was distraught. In consultation with the court astrologer, he got the prince married to a girl with a very lucky horoscope, hoping that her destiny would overpower the boy's. The girl was intelligent and showed no remorse in marrying a man doomed to die soon.

Four days after the wedding, the prince was to turn sixteen. It was the thirteenth day of the waning moon, and the night was poorly lit. The young bride piled all her jewelry as well as shiny gold coins and vessels near the door entrance of her bedroom and lit the room with lamps, so there would be no dark spots. She sat on the bed with her husband and sung songs to him, recited poems and narrated stories to prevent him from falling asleep.

Yama, the Lord of Death, came at night. Slithering in the form of a serpent, he slid under the doorway. The many lamp lights reflecting on the shiny coins and mounds of ornaments blinded him and he sat on the pile of wealth. He heard the soulful singing and was mesmerized by the tunes of the newlywed princess and listened to her poetry and stories. The hours flew by and soon, it was dawn; the ill-fated hour had passed; Yama quickly slithered out the door as he had come. The little princess had saved her husband. People all over India celebrate this legend even today by buying ornaments or vessels on the thirteenth day of the waning moon, on the festival Dhanteras and light lamps all through the night as a prayer to Yama."

Rajat smiled at the tale, and said, "I must buy something for my wife. I know that your stories are leading me to buy, but you are right, I am indeed lucky and she will be happy to get a gift from me."

At the store, he had to remove his shoes outside and sat on the mattresses on the floor. Prabod stood outside and sipped a cup of tea that the shop owner had miraculously arranged for all of them; the salesmen started to show the collection quickly, one after the other. The shopkeeper seemed indefatigable in showing sarees to Rajat, insisting that he see some of his specialties. He seemed tireless although Rajat tried meekly and hopelessly to stop him from opening any more bundles of sarees.

It was a smorgasbord of silken fabrics and colors with exquisite work on them and Rajat felt a bit like the serpent in the story that he had just heard on his way to the shop, bewildered with all the glitter and shine, unable to make any move.

"Do not open more," he said but the shopkeeper waved a hand in the air and said, "Do not worry, sir, it is an honor to show you our latest collection. Why do you worry? You are under no pressure to buy anything if you do not wish to." He threw a saree to an attendant and said, "Show us how good it will look draped," and Rajat was horrified when the man began to open the saree, fold pleats into it and tuck parts over his pants and then drape the colorful fabric around himself. Rajat felt a mild disgust, wondering why the man would don on the saree, he could not see it as salesmanship nor was he amused by it. He could not put a finger to what exactly bothered him, but he had a similar feeling last night during dinner when he saw the dance recital in the dining hall of the hotel. There had been a Kathak recital by two artistes; they danced in tandem beautifully. The hotel had placed dining tables around the little inner courtyard; and in the center was this young couple dancing scenes from the scriptures. Rajat had felt a mild distaste seeing the man with bright lipstick and strong eyeliner exaggerating his facial features, but what had disturbed him the most was the feminine movements and expressions. While the other guest had clapped and applauded, Rajat had eaten the set meal quickly and had departed.

Sitting in the shop, he saw the man with the half-worn saree sway gently so that the gold embroidery and sequins captured the light and shimmered and the crystals twinkled and felt the same discomfort as he had had last evening during dinner. Rajat squirmed a little and said, "Please ask him to remove the saree." He knew he had said it a little sharper than he had intended to, somewhere Dr Mehrotra appeared in his mind and chided him to be more tactful, and in apology, he said to the shop owner, "I'll take that saree for my wife."

The shopkeeper beamed and the attendant smiled, thrilled at the early morning sale.

Rajat, guided by Prabod, made his way back to the hotel. "You have indeed made a fantastic purchase and he gave a good discount too," said Prabod. "I am sure your wife will be very pleased with it. Let me hold the shopping bag for you until we reach the hotel," he said, taking the jute bag from Rajat's hand.

That afternoon, Rajat was to experience the now all too familiar sense of unpleasantness again for the third time. At lunch, he sat in the open veranda of the hotel, facing the river, the sunlight on his body feeling like a protective coat from the winter air. It was Sunday afternoon and the hotel had a live performer on a small makeshift stage. Rajat was enjoying the lilting songs and he looked up at the singer to applaud. He gasped for he had expected a woman but the performer on the stage looked decidedly male. He peered to see the singer and realized it was a woman, but she looked like a young boy, her hair, her clothing, her body language was masculine and her voice androgynous. He really wondered why this unpalatable experience was recurring for he was used to seeing effeminate men or masculine women at the hospital; it was surprising that he should feel such a strong sense of distaste in Varanasi. He changed his seat, so his back faced the stage; he ate quickly and went to the lobby to wait for Amrit, Surya and the guide to take them for the tour of the gulleys of Varanasi.

CHAPTER 6

VARANASI, DAY TWO, AFTERNOON THE GHATS AND GULLEYS TOUR

"Death is not the opposite of life, but a part of it."

–Haruki Murakami

Dharam led the three of them into the tiny lanes of Varanasi, up the irregular steps. Amrit looked at Dharam's limp and asked him, "Is it okay for you to climb the steps?"

The guide smiled warmly and said, "Do not worry. I have lived with this bad leg for many years now and am used to it. I can go up these stairs blindfolded if needed."

Dharam guided them in the gulleys explaining the stories and said, "A lot happens in Varanasi in these narrow lanes, and they all eventually lead to the ghats. To feel the essence of the city, you need to walk in these alleyways."

They were amazed to see how small and winding the gulleys were. Often, they had to sidestep cow dung in their path; sometimes, they jumped onto the side as a motorbike approached them, totally ignoring their presence and blowing its horn incessantly. There were cycles and garbage dumps blocking their paths as they walked; they looked in wonderment at life in the oldest living city, an assault to all their five senses. They passed houses, painted in bright colors, vivid and sometimes garish, little alcoves carved in the walls, each housing a tiny deity. They would peep into the houses to see the residents carrying out their daily chores and Amrit said, "It is like peering into the soul of India." Although they would sidestep cows eating garbage that had been dumped from an overhead window callously, without attention to passersby below, Amrit felt the city was alluring. "There is something real about the city," he said to the others and Surya and Rajat nodded. In spite of the filth, noise and grime, the city had a strange sense of orderliness to it in the madness, perfection in its randomness, a sense of the ethereal in its earthiness. Rajat was surprised that he was enjoying the city so much. He had reluctantly embarked on his solo vacation in Varanasi with very little expectation. During the conference, he toyed with the idea of returning home, but he was glad he had not canceled this part of the trip. Therefore, he was pleasantly surprised as he found himself actually loving the holiday, the company of two strangers, although he knew he would never meet them again, the calming sight of the Ganges, the informative guides and their interesting stories. Rajat would hang on to each word, asking questions on each place and clicking photos that he hoped to show his family when he returned home. He liked the time alone in his room, to be able to lie down peacefully without a routine. He understood why these solo holidays were a good way to connect with oneself.

They reached a junction; Dharam crossed the road and the others followed to enter another Varanasi sight.

"Where have we reached?" asked Rajat.

Before Dharam could reply, Surya commented, "I feel Shiva everywhere." The others turned to him and found him standing with his arms outstretched as if absorbing vibes from the air; trancelike, he repeated, "I feel Shiva everywhere."

Dharam stared at Surya but answered Rajat's question. "We have reached Manikarnika Ghat," he said softly, his gaze yet fixed on Surya. He pulled out some money and got them an entrance ticket to the burning ghat. They stood on the viewing gallery, overlooking the cremation grounds just below them. It was located next to the waters of the Ganges and they could see local children splashing in the water. The mud in the ghat was a strange mixture, of dirty brown and all shades of gray from white ash to charred wood. A smell permeated, the peculiar smell of burning, of ghee mixed with sandalwood, wafting and filling the air, making it thick with the scents of ancient rituals. There were three lit pyres, the families of the dead standing with their heads bowed. One man was crying loudly and he was quickly led away for wailing was forbidden. Nearby lay the preparations for another pyre being set. The workers moved around unemotionally, doing their tasks professionally. It was mesmerizing, in a way, affecting nearly all of the senses. Rajat looked at Surya and saw that his companion was lost in some kind of trance; he was somewhere far away, a look of dejection and hopelessness on his face. Surya's shoulders sagged and his face had turned sallow. Dharam cleared his throat and Rajat and Amrit turned their gaze from the pyres to look at him but Surya remained transfixed, his gaze locked on the scene. "Let me tell you the history of this ghat called Manikarnika," said the guide, "and then you all can spend some time here if you wish. But do remember, no photographs are allowed."

Surya joined them as they moved closer, all eyes and ears on Dharam as he spoke. Ashes from the pyres burning below were eddying in the air, flying around them. The weather was cold, the sky overcast, and they were transposed to another world, to another time as Dharam started the tale of Manikarnika.

"We are at the holy site of the forever burning fires. They call them the perennial fires. It is said that if these flames go off, then the world will end. There are different stories about the origins of the ghat and the *kund*, but I will tell you the one from the Puranas."

"What is a kund?" asked Rajat.

"Ah, it is the well you can see over there – it is supposed to have been made by Vishnuji himself. Long, long ago, probably in another cycle of Creation."

"I am sorry to interrupt again but how do they know that this happened in another cycle of Creation? And was Varanasi there even at that time?" said Rajat, unable to control himself. Throughout the trip, he had listened to the guides speak of many things that contradicted his scientific training and sensibilities, deciding to go with the flow as the good Doctor Mehrotra had explained to him. Sometimes, he was unable to control himself.

"Rajatji, Kashi is a city that will never be destroyed. Even in Pralaya, which is the dissolution of the Universe, Kashi, our city of light and liberation, will survive as it is protected by Shivji. Anyways, let me continue with my story. I will give you only a gist as it is a long one.

Mata Sati was the daughter of King Daksh, a very arrogant and powerful king and she had been born after many prayers. Naradji would often visit his kingdom and would tell the little princess, Sati, stories of Shivji. As she grew up, she decided that she would marry only Shivji and no one else.

She went into the jungle to pray for Shiv Bhagwanji's attention. Her penances were rigorous and severe, with single-minded prayer and concentration for her Lord. Shivji was an ascetic, a nomad and an aimless wanderer but he could no longer ignore Mata Sati and her devoted prayer, so he agreed to marry her and become a householder."

"Vairagya," said Surya, "that was the word they explained yesterday on the evening boat ride. Shiva was a vairagya."

Dharam looked at him and continued, "King Daksh, Mata Sati's father was extremely upset that his precious daughter would marry Shivji, whom he considered good for nothing. He tried to dissuade Mata Sati but finally agreed; consequently, he cut off ties with his daughter.

Mata Sati and Shivji lived happily in Mount Kailash. One day, Mata Sati heard that her father was performing a big yagna." Dharam paused as he looked around. Surya was yet in a daze, apparently listening to the story but looking far away.

"What is a yagna?" asked Rajat.

"Yagna is a ritual, like a prayer that is performed with a fire for a very specific reason. It was a very big one, conducted by Bhriguji, one of the great sages; all the Devas and Rishis were attending. Mata Sati got to know about this big ceremony that her father was conducting; she knew everyone would be there and she wanted to go too. 'Let us go,' she said to her husband. Shivji shook his head and said, 'We have not been invited.'

Mata Sati laughed; 'A woman does not have to be invited to her father's house,' she exclaimed. 'Besides, it will be nice to meet my mother and sisters again and all my relatives.'

'I will not be going,' said Shivji flatly, 'and I don't think you should go either.'

'I would like to go,' said Mata Sati despondently, looking at her husband forlornly.

Shivji agreed and sent Mata Sati with Nandi and a couple of bodyguards to her father's house. Thus, Mata Sati left Mount Kailash and reached her paternal home, full of excitement and anticipation. When she reached, she saw the place was fully decorated and festive; she rushed inside to hug her father and mother and take their blessings. She saw her father observe her enter but ignore her and continue talking to the others; Mata Sati wondered why her father would snub her and her heart began to beat faster. *Maybe he is busy,* she reasoned to herself and waited nearby for him to acknowledge her but he remained aloof and distant. She decided to approach him and went up to him to touch his feet and hug him. 'Father,' she said, 'I have come to be with you and the family.' However, Daksh looked at his daughter reproachfully and insulted her. 'Why would you come when you were not even invited? Is it so unbearable to stay with that useless son-in-law of mine?' Having said this, Daksh grew angrier and lost all control, spewing insult upon insult on his daughter's husband, the mighty Shivji.

Poor Mata Sati could neither bear the harsh words, nor the ignominy toward her beloved; she covered her ears at first, then wept, finally she grew angry and cursed

Daksh. She then leaped into the yagna fire and immolated herself.

When Nandi and the other bodyguards reported it to Shivji, he came down from Mt Kailash in a fury. He saw the burned body of Mata Sati and got enraged. First, he beheaded King Daksh in anger and then carried his wife's charred body with him in sadness. Full of anguish, he wandered about, not able to vent his sorrow or his anger as he kept gazing at the inert, lifeless body of his wife. Finally, he decided to perform the dance of death, the famous *Tandav* that would destroy Creation. All the gods grew worried that Creation will come to an end unless Shivji releases his anger and Vishnuji came to the rescue; he sent his whirling serrated disc, the Sudarshan Chakra, which dismembered the body of Mata Sati into fifty-one pieces. These fell in different parts of the country, and each of these locations became a place of worship. The earrings fell in Varanasi at this spot and hence it is called Manikarnika."

Rajat was surprised at himself enjoying Indian mythology, although he did not understand many of the terms being used. He did not believe actively in religion yet but the tales being narrated were so colorful and imaginative, so full of real-life emotions that they were enthralling. The gods in these stories were alive, unlike the ones in the little temple that Nayana prayed to at home every day. Amrit had shielded his eyes from the spray of ash that was descending upon them and settling on their hair and shoulders. "Surya, you said you sensed

Shiva when we entered this ghat, well you were right." Dharam looked at Surya and said, "This is indeed the ghat of Shivji."

They left the top viewing gallery and Dharam limped towards the lower level. "If you wish to see the Eternal Fire, then we can go to the lower level. This fire has been burning for more than five thousand years."

"We would certainly like to see it," said Surya enthusiastically. He was being drawn to this spot. It was eerie that he felt totally possessed by the ambiance of Manikarnika. He had a sense of déjà vu, a feeling that he had been here several times before; it felt like he was returning home. There was a comfort in being here. They hastened down the uneven steps, closer to the funeral fires, but yet just one level above them. There was a small open furnace with burning wooden logs. It was mesmerizing, for the glow was an eerie neon orange, the logs blazed in parts and were pitch black in others where the soot had covered it or gray in spots with ash. There were no roaring flames. "This is the Eternal Fire," said Dharam; the others looked at him as they heard a sigh and wondered if their guide had sighed but it was just a silent hiss from the Eternal Fire that burned in front of them. "Shivji came down looking for the earrings of Mata Sati," he said, "and when he could not find them, he leashed his unabated anger at the city. This part was a forest and the fire from his third eye burned it down. At that point, the Rishis in the forest prayed to Shivji to direct his anger on a spot where it could come to some use and this is where it was directed. Thus, was born the Eternal Flame, straight from Shivji's third eye and lights all the funeral pyres at this ghat." Dharam instinctively touched the spot between his brows and the trio stared at the captivating fire in front of them. "That is why this city is also called Avimukta, the city that Shiva will never forsake, the city where Shiva will always live. Come on, let us go out this way to see the pyres," said the guide and they turned to leave. Amrit saw Surya staring at the flame, hypnotized and he touched him on the shoulder and said, "Surya, come on, let us go."

Reluctantly, Surya followed Amrit out to the open, to the cacophony of Manikarnika. "If you all wish to stay here for a few moments, you can sit here. I will be waiting outside. Take your time; there is no need to hurry."

"I will come with you," said Rajat, striding behind Dharam. Amrit and Surya sat separately on the tall steps at the ghat, very near the burning pyres.

Amrit stared at the roaring flames, the Dom men using their sticks to prod the fires. The assault on his senses dissolved as all he could see was the fire. The flames felt alive, dancing their wild dance, throwing themselves up in the air and then devouring everything below them. He remembered the death of his father where he had gone mechanically to light the pyre of his dead father at the crematorium. A tear rolled down his eyes; a relationship between father and son, such a vital and precious one, had been denied to him. He knew it was not his place to forgive or not forgive; he realized it had just happened, uncontrolled by him or his Baba; he was neither victim nor his father, the perpetrator. They had both lost something precious. A mild whisper of repentance slithered within him; he wished he had gotten to know his estranged father better. His gaze moved from the flames on to the Ganges as it silently flowed, soothing the eyes after the intensity of the fire. *It will all pass; it has already flowed long back. Everything will keep flowing*, it seemed to say to him. Amrit wiped the tears with the corner of his sleeve and gave a mild smile. *Goodbye Baba*, he said to himself. He continued to sit for a few more minutes, knowing the voice in his head at Aai's death was his Baba's voice asking him to come to Varanasi to say his final goodbye. They both needed closure and he was glad it happened for he never realized the burden of estrangement that he had carried in his heart all along, never understood how the repressions of his missing father had played out inside of him. Slowly he rose and made his way outside, looking out for Dharam and Rajat.

Surya sat a little away staring at the flames of burning fires. The city, the ghat, the people and the sounds ceased to exist and he felt himself spiraling inside an inescapable void, an emptiness within himself. He seemed to have toppled into another world, through the blazing fire, into a space of no color. He felt immensely lonely, a feeling of dread and unimaginable fear seeping into his veins and numbing him, closing all reason and reality. He saw the burning pyres of his parents, who were both alive yet. He knew he had come here before, probably eons ago, for he saw a fire burning his dead body lifetimes ago. So, he oscillated in the future and past, juxtaposed in between, dangling within no time. His heart beat un-rhythmically and a tear rolled down his face, hot from the funeral fires. He tried to get up to leave but his strength and willpower had deserted him; he felt old, thousands of years old, like a tree that had been rooted to view the surreal and sublime panorama of Manikarnika. Flying ash stuck on his wet cheeks, creating stains, aging him even further. Slowly, he wiped his face with his palms; a man seated next to him said slowly, "All of us must go some time; only the name of God will remain. *Ram naam satya hai*," said the man in Hindi, and got up. He stretched his hand out to help Surya to stand; Surya grabbed the man's hand and heaved himself up, out of the abyss, through the void.

Outside, Amrit and Rajat were patiently waiting with Dharam.

"Varanasi itself is overwhelming," said Amrit, "but this was something else altogether. It is only at Manikarnika that one faces death head-on, so directly and nakedly. It leaves you feeling that you have entered an ancient world, something that is too intense to be affected by you. You feel helpless in a way, as if it is preparing you for a journey, the eternal one."

"Yes, it is a lot to take in. But you have nothing to worry about, sir," said Dharam.

Amrit looked at the guide quizzically and said, "And why is that?"

Dharam smiled and said, "Your very name says A-Mrityu…one who can never die. You are eternal like Varanasi, sir."

"Ha-ha," said Amrit, "Don't say that. I am not here to stay forever. By the way, where is Surya? Did he not come out yet?"

"He is yet inside," said Dharam, "Being at Manikarnika can be quite an overwhelming experience as you probably know. Some people need more time at this ghat."

"Do we have time in our schedule?"

"Yes, do not worry, as we have enough time for the evening aarthi. Let us stand here on the side and wait for Suryaji. I will keep an eye so that we do not miss him."

"Which city allows visitors to witness cremations twenty-four hours a day? What is this strange city?" said Rajat to Dharam, "I just cannot reconcile with it."

"It is a special city," said the guide, "but what is it that you cannot reconcile?"

"What is there not to reconcile? For one, on one side there are bodies burning at Manikarnika, the son with his head shorn of hair, the relatives quietly weeping in sorrow and just a few meters from them are the local children frolicking in the Ganges. There are shops selling holy products and outside their shutters is garbage piled up.

This is the city of the pure but yet an assault on all the senses in terms of smells, sights and sounds. You would expect the holiest city of the world to be peaceful but Varanasi is a cacophony of sounds, full of smells and constantly moving crowds. I agree it has a different energy but it is full of irreconcilable contrasts."

Dharam smiled and then looked at Rajat in his eyes. Rajat felt himself swimming in the gaze and felt everything around him blur for a split second before he shook himself. Dharam continued his stare and then said, "Life is full of dualities."

"What do you mean?" asked Rajat, perplexed and curious.

"There is black and there is white. The cold winter morning is a contrast to the hot summer afternoon in Varanasi."

"But what does that have to do with Varanasi?"

"It does not have to do with Varanasi. It has to do with you, it has to do with everyone else," said Dharam slowly, softly but firmly, his eyes yet locked with Rajat's. "Dualities like up and down are not opposing concepts. We need one to understand the other. Dryness is nothing but an absence of wetness."

"I do not understand it," said Rajat, his voice full of puzzlement.

"Take life and death – on and off – like two switches – life and death. We are at Manikarnika, the ghat of the dead. But unless there is no death, you will have no worth for your breath, no value for life. If you lived forever, life would lose its charm, its immediacy, its complete meaning. We value life because we know death exists."

"Ah, that is an interesting thought. I never thought of it this way. I love how the generalization sums it all up."

"It is not a general statement," said Dharam firmly, but quietly, "it is specific to each of us."

"How is that so?" asked Rajat. Amrit and he both were transfixed, intently listening to Dharam.

Dharam then took a deep sigh and said, "There is one duality that you need to work out especially since you are here in Varanasi. If there is one God that dominates this city, it is Shivji, whose raging fire gave rise to the Eternal Flame in Manikarnika. But he too is part of the duality. He is Shiva, his counterpart feminine energy is Shakti."

"But energy is never classified as male and female," said Rajat, "I have studied science and I can tell you for sure that energy is never divided by gender."

Dharam smiled. "You're right," he said, "Energy is not the duality of male or female, for gender is only a manmade construct, Shiva is both male and female. He comprises an amalgamation of the two."

Amrit piped in, "So is it that we are both man and woman inside us?"

"Yes," said Dharam. "There is only one life force and it is without gender, without age and without physical form. All dualities exist within us. Every part of the Universe is within us."

"Then why is there such a distinct polarization toward heterosexual relationships?" murmured Amrit softly, as if talking to himself.

Rajat glanced at Amrit; Dharam said, "Society has its own rules to serve its existence. In Shiva's eyes, there is no difference if you are with a man or a woman, for Shiva is both male and female, Shiva and Shakti."

Amrit smiled inwardly. This was exactly how he had thought of gender and God all along but now it seemed to make logical sense as well. He missed Gagan tremendously especially after his final farewell to his father at Manikarnika Ghat; he needed him here now. The short but insightful talk with Dharam made him think of him with even more urgency. "I need to make a personal phone call," he said, "I will be standing near those steps; call me when Surya returns." He stepped aside and dialed Gagan's phone.

Dharam in the meantime continued speaking to Rajat. "Have you recognized the energy of Shakti in your life?"

"Who exactly is Shakti?" asked Rajat, a bit confused, but very interested. Deep within him, he knew that there was something that was true and primordially correct in what the guide was saying. He needed to get to the bottom of it. His heart was beating just a bit faster, the hair on his body stood up, signaling fear or euphoria or a reaction to a strong emotion, his sympathetic nervous system sending out adrenaline signals to flee or fight.

A man selling tea approached them and Dharam asked for two *kulhads* of chai. In Benaras, it was rightfully assumed that two people talking together for some time would welcome a cup of tea. Rajat was not certain whether he really wanted a cup but it seemed to be a good idea to sip on something with sugar after the sights at Manikarnika and on hearing the topics that Dharam was discussing.

"You asked me who Shakti is," said Dharam, staring into his cup of chai. He lifted his hand and took a sip. "Well, she has a hundred and eight names. She can be Nitya, the eternal or Sumangali, the one who brings good luck; Kanta who is beautiful or Kamakshi who awakens desire by her eyes; brilliant in Shobha and giver of prosperity as Mahalaxmi, Lalita the charmer and Mridani who gives pleasure, she is sweet as honey in form of Madhumati and the Goddess of Speech as Bharti. There are so many forms in which we know Shakti."

"How do you even know so many names?" said Rajat.

"You are a doctor and we wonder how you know the names of so many bones, muscles and nerves," replied Dharam with an impish smile.

Rajat laughed. "That is true," he said.

"Like the bones and muscles, Shakti too lies with each of us. Each of the hundred and eight names is within each of us."

Rajat kept quiet and Dharam understood that Rajat was not a believer in his words.

"We have to wait for Suryaji," said Dharam. "I think he will take a while inside. Manikarnika arouses strange emotions in different people, but everyone who comes here has come for a reason. It is a blessing that gets them here, whether they realize it or not. While Amritji is talking on the phone and Suryaji has not yet come, may I suggest that you visit a small temple in this same square? It is a temple of Shakti, it's called the Visalakshi temple and it is just behind that wall there," said Dharam pointing to a small temple. Rajat looked at where Dharam was pointing and saw a small beautifully carved multicolored structure.

"It looks like the temples from South India," he said.

"Indeed, you are correct, sir. It has been restored by the Chettiar community from Tamil Nadu. If you remember the story I narrated near the Eternal Flame, Vishnu's Sudarshan Chakra cut the body into many parts and the earrings of Sati fell in Varanasi. The temple that I am showing you is the exact spot where her earrings fell and they have built a temple for Mata Shakti. The priest inside will tell you her face fell in Varanasi to aggrandize the temple; he will even claim that her face is within the back of the statue."

"So, should I go behind the statue?" asked Rajat innocently. "You see, I do not know much about the protocol of temples. My place of worship is the hospital.

Please come with me to guide me there and you can tell me more about the temple and Shakti."

"What you call your temple is the true place of worship; for more genuine prayers are whispered in hospitals than temples," said Dharam. "You are not going to worship the statue; go and sit there for a few minutes and think of the Shakti within you and with you. I better wait here for Suryaji. He should be coming out soon. You go ahead and we will wait for you. It's a small temple – it should not take you too much time."

Rajat walked to the temple nearby. Too many names and too many different functions of each Goddess, he thought, but then decided to sit in the temple and think of them as different aspects of feminine energy as suggested by the guide. He removed his shoes and as he entered temple, the priest approached him and as predicted said, "Welcome to the home of Sati's face and earring. The temple is dedicated to Visalakshi Devi, which means to the Goddess with large eyes. Rajat stopped and stared at the priest and said, "The Goddess with large eyes?"

The priest preened with the sudden interest of the visitor and he said, "This is the temple of the Goddess with large eyes; Visalakshi means Nayana, big eyes." It was at this point in time that it suddenly began to make sense to him – Universal Energy, the Goddess, large eyes, Nayana – his wife's name. The pandit kept talking but Rajat had zoned out. He heard the priest talk in the background, "Think of the nine goddesses of Navratri.

Durga, the destroyer of evil; Bhadrakali, the dark Goddess who is helpful and generous; Amba, the universal mother; Annapoorna, the Goddess of Food; Sarvamngala, who prays for us and our well-being; Mookambika, the mother, and Bhairavi or Chandi, who looks fierce, she is wrathful at the enemy but tender towards the ones she loves and cares for." Rajat picked up a few of the characteristics but did not register any names.

He removed his spectacles and wiped them. His head started to spin with these names and he excused himself. "I need to sit and contemplate," he said to the priest. He walked slowly and sat in front of the dark garlanded statue, which indeed had eyes that were large and all-knowing. He closed his eyes and started to contemplate; accepting the thoughts and images as they came. At first, he visualised his family and as he saw them, he realized that he had been blessed with feminine energy surrounding him. Since he had not tapped into the feminine energy within himself, it had manifested all around him – his mother, his wife, his daughter – all different aspects of Divine Shakti. Each would protect him, nurture him, fight off everyone else for him, feed him, and pray for his well-being. Then, he saw his father and gasped for he comprehended clearly for the first time that his father too would do the same for him; his father too had nurtured him and fed him and prayed for him. He understood that the energy was the same in all men and women, uniform, unbiased of gender. He realized that he too had Shakti inside him, pervading every cell for he too nurtured his patients and took care of their illnesses. He now knew that it was ignorance that had made him uncomfortable with the androgynous singer that afternoon, or the saree wearing salesman or the distaste he had felt the previous night when he saw the male Kathak dancer. For the first time, he folded his palms together and thanked the Goddess with the large eyes, for expanding his limited vision, for actually opening his eyes to the Shakti that permeated him, engulfed him and surrounded him. He said a silent prayer and got up light-heartedly, and immensely happy.

He left the temple and walked back to where Dharam and Amrit were standing. He saw Surya walking toward them too. "You were at the Manikarnika Ghat for a long time," he remarked to Surya.

Surya lifted his head to reply. His eyes were red but no words left his lips. Amrit looked at Surya and said, "It looks like the ash has given you an allergy," he remarked, looking at Surya's runny nose and reddened eyes.

Surya tried to fashion a reply but his face twisted and contorted and he covered it with his palms. He burst out crying – it was a strange sound, something like a mixture between a braying, snorting and wailing. Amrit instinctively put his arm around him and guided him to sit on the steps on the river bank. Surya would not stop sobbing, his hands on his face; Rajat handed him a handkerchief and patted him slowly on the back. They did not know what to do; they had been taken by complete surprise at the turn of events; they were worried and yet curious and looked at each other silently for answers that the others may have.

In a few minutes, Surya stopped and wiped his face; he looked at his companions and smiled weakly. "I'm fine," he managed to say. Dharam got a bottle of water and Surya opened it clumsily and poured it over his face to wash the stains of ash mixed with tears.

"It is alright," said Dharam gently, "this ghat has an effect on many people." Surya tried to get up from the steps but fumbled.

"Don't get up yet," said Amrit, "Let us sit here for a couple of minutes more. We have the time."

They sat down beside Surya and looked at the placid river flowing by. Dharam spoke somberly, repeating the emotion that the stranger inside had said, "All of us who come to Earth must go."

"It is not that," said Surya awkwardly. He wanted to explain what had happened to him at the ghat but found himself unable to express the strange emotions that he had undergone.

"Normally we do not think about death in our daily life, but the truth is different from reality. We forget that from the moment we are born, we start our journey toward death. Some walk slowly, others run toward it, some skip and dance their way there, and others crawl. We all are walking in only one direction, and yet we forget where we are going," said Dharam, "Manikarnika is a reminder and so it affects us deeply, so don't get so upset sir, we all must go some time."

"It is a strange thought," said Rajat, "but very true. I really never thought of life and death so intertwined."

"They are not opposites but extensions of each other, as I explained to you when we spoke on dualities," said Dharam.

"Maybe the ghat teaches us to enjoy the journey," said Surya.

"There have been many who have had visions at Manikarnika," said Dharam. "Sri Ramakrishna, who founded the mission, said he saw Shivji when he visited this ghat. He saw him covered with ash, his hair matted and wild; he would go from the funeral pyre and whisper the mantra of liberation in the ear of each dead body. And Mata Sati would untie the body from the worldly chains."

"What is this mantra of liberation?" asked Amrit, his voice full of curiosity and anticipation.

"Well," said Dharam, "we will have to wait for Shivji to whisper it in our ears to know. Some people say it is the universal sound 'Aum', which has no beginning or end, others say '*Ram naam*' is the mantra. I really do not know," said Dharam sheepishly looking at the disappointment written across Amrit's face.

"What is liberation?" asked Rajat.

"Ah, that is the fundamental question," said Dharam, "that all of us seek the answer to. It is called moksh. I am not wise enough to explain it but I can give you a small introduction. As I said, life and death are just cycles of journeys and transformations. My friend, Sreenivasrao, used to say, death is not a punishment but is a part of the sequence of life. Death is not the final end; but is a passage or a doorway to other possibilities that might exist thereafter. It is like getting into a new dress, discarding the old and worn out, and going about fresh business." And he laughed and said, "As my mother used to put it, 'Death is like being shifted from one breast to the other breast of the mother. The baby feels lost for a short instant, but not for long.' So, you see sir, moksh is liberation from that never-ending cycle."

"And people come to Varanasi to fast track into moksh, is it?" said Rajat smiling, which was surprising because normally he would have broken into a tirade against the concept of rebirth and the lack of proof that it happened, that life came into being when a sperm and an ova fused and ended when a person died. He was excited and happy to be here, and he kept thinking that he must travel more often. Dr Mehrotra was right. He would call him once he returned home and thank him.

Surya got up, without fumbling this time. He seemed much better, cheerful, and in fact, even, light-headed. "Let's go," he said, "I am fine," and he smiled broadly.

They arose and started their way out of this surreal and sublime ghat and into the city with blaring horns, into the alleys with stray dogs and garbage eating cows, into the chaos and the frenetic.

CHAPTER 7

VARANASI, DAY TWO, NIGHT

"What are men? Mortal Gods. What are Gods? Immortal Men."

–Heraclitus

Dharam left them at Deena Chat Bhandar on Surya's request. Beej and Tushar at his office had given Surya a list of eateries to visit when he was in Varanasi. The three men were surprised at the narrow street on which the restaurant was located. It was more of a stall than a restaurant, with a little sitting space, very unpretentious and basic, yet very crowded. Rajat wondered if it was hygienic to eat in such a place but remembered the dualities of the city and decided to risk it. He clicked photographs on his phone for he was sure that Nayana would never believe that he would dine in such an eatery, snapping pictures of the huge *tawa* with *tikkis* frying in them and *chaat* mashed on the side. Locals on motorbikes, their horns blaring, knitting their route between ambling cows and sleeping street dogs passed them as the three men stood in the alley waiting for their order to be accepted. Around the food stall, were shops selling every conceivable item, their tiny boutiques lit very brightly and their wares prominently displayed.

They ordered *Tamatar Chaat* for it was the specialty of the city; they watched the man skillfully mix things that they never would have imagined combined in a dish, flavors that would tickle all the taste buds at the same time. Surya took his plate with anticipated relish, Rajat with caution and Amrit with guarded enthusiasm; they took the first bite, wrinkled their nose and looked at each other. They could not decide if they liked it or not. "It is certainly different," said Rajat, "I have not eaten anything like this." The others laughed for they felt the same and then the three of them went in for a second bite and it was then that the flavor overpowered their senses.

After sampling and sharing various dishes at the chaat shop, they were pleasantly surprised at the low bill. "We now have to go for *Malai* toast and chai," said Amrit looking at the list on his phone sent by Gagan; they sauntered to the next stop. "I've eaten too much," said Surya, rubbing his stomach, "I don't think I can have a toast, but warm chai will be welcome." The weather had turned colder and after the chai, the three returned to the hotel.

"Do you want to sit on the verandah?" asked Amrit, not wanting to part from Surya yet.

"I am afraid I must go," said Rajat, "for I need to pack. I am leaving early morning tomorrow." He was excited to get back home, he wanted to meet his wife and daughter, and he wanted to hug his mother and especially his father. He wanted to meet Dr Mehrotra and show him the photographs of his first solo trip.

"I need to do some reading," said Surya, "and then I will be stepping out again."

"Where are you going?" asked Amrit curiously

"I think I will visit Manikarnika once again," said Surya flatly. Amrit looked sideways at Rajat, wondering if it was wise for Surya to go to the ghat alone at night, where he had had a meltdown.

"But it is dark now," suggested Rajat, "maybe you can go tomorrow."

"I have to meet someone there," said Surya mysteriously and turned to go to his room.

At about nine o' clock that evening, Surya walked out of the hotel to go to Manikarnika. It was a dark night; the sky was clear with many twinkling stars and the air was heavy and cold. He had worn a sweater to protect himself against the chill but he wished he had carried a cap as well. He quickened his pace to keep himself warm, his hands in his pocket. A breeze wafted from the river and a light shiver ran through him. He was surprised that the steps were dotted with people for he had expected the city to be barren at this time of the night, but then realized that it was not so late after all.

He passed a couple of boys who were sitting on the riverfront, one strumming a guitar and the other singing.

Normally he would have liked to stand in the shadows and listen to them but tonight he walked purposefully. He was sure that someone was waiting for him, he was literally being called to Manikarnika and he started to walk a little faster.

When he reached Manikarnika, he was not surprised to see it busy as it normally was. He knew that the funeral pyres burned all day and through the night and had been burning since time immemorial. No one glanced at him, everyone was busy with their own work and he walked to the lower deck.

"Suryaji, what are you doing here?" asked a voice from the side.

Surya turned and peered; he saw Dharam, their guide standing there. His body seemed to be gleaming with the light from a nearby pyre burning and the tattoo of the bull on his arm appeared to be outlined in fire and alive.

Surya stood nonplussed, not knowing what to answer. He tried to stammer a coherent reply but Dharam came closer to him and gently said, "Does this have something to do with what happened here earlier today?"

Surya looked at him blankly and nodded. Many thoughts arose within him but he seemed to have lost his capacity to reason and articulate. He now knew why he had been called, he knew who it was that had called him there and strangely he was not afraid. He saw a bier lying close by on the ground, it was a makeshift bed made for the dead, with the precision of ancient texts. Only bamboo sticks made the framework, tied with coir cords, tightly bound to support the weight of a corpse. Surya bent down and sat on the bamboo bed meant for the un-living. "Stop," said Dharam, "that is not meant for you. It's for the deceased. What are you doing?"

Surya lay down on the bed and looked peacefully at Dharam.

"I know who you are," he said dramatically, "and I know you have called me here. My time has come, so take me with you. I am prepared."

"What are you talking about?" said Dharam, a look of shock and surprise on his face. "I think you should get up fast before the Dom people come after you. This is no joking matter and I really don't understand what you are talking about."

"I know you are Yama, the Lord of Death," said Surya.

"What!" exclaimed Dharam.

Surya continued lying on the bed made of bamboo and spoke, full of earnestness, "I have been thinking about it these past two hours and googled a lot about it as well and it all falls in place. I know you are none other than Yama."

"Suryaji, let us talk about this outside. I assure you I am not Yamraj. Please get up," he said stretching his hands toward the supine Surya.

On seeing the extended hand, Surya shrank back. "Is it time now? Have you come to take me?" he asked, holding his hands tight, close to his body.

A man from the Dom came and angrily asked, "Dharamji, who is this man and why is he lying on our bier? We have prepared it for a newly arrived body and now it is polluted." Behind him, another Dom man poked a roaring fire, to shatter a skull. They heard a crackling sound, the flames rose higher, throwing up embers and ash.

"Don't be upset," said Dharam, gently mollifying the man, "Suryaji is from Mumbai and is a client of mine. He wanted to test a theory; he is just getting up."

"He will have to pay for this bed now as we cannot use it," demanded the man, not placated.

"You can sprinkle *Ganga Jal* on it and it will be purer than what it was," said Dharam calmly, knowing that the argument he had made was infallible in Varanasi. "C'mon," he said extending his hand again to Surya, "Let's go."

The man from the Dom muttered under his breath while Surya caught Dharam's hand and pulled himself up, looking meek and a bit foolish.

"Now what is it that you were saying about me being Yama?"

Surya looked a little sheepish. "It was probably just my imagination running wild," he said. "Since I have come to Manikarnika, I have not been myself. The experience left me thinking about death and in my confused state, I saw a pattern."

"What kind of pattern?" asked Dharam, his voice puzzled and his brow full of inquiry.

"Well, small things but when they all connect, they seem to be too uncanny. Your name, for one, is Dharam, and Yama is called Dharamraj often as he is the upholder of justice."

"Ha-ha, but you cannot go by a name, for then you would be the Sun God himself."

"Yes, I agree but then there was the tattoo of a buffalo on your hand. Traditionally, Yama is shown riding a buffalo, it is his vehicle." Dharam looked at his tattoo and smiled. "It is not a buffalo," he said, with a broad grin, "it's a bull. I have it because my sun sign is Taurus. My parents were big followers in astrology and I grew up believing in it too. I got this tattoo when I was in college."

"When I entered the ghat and I saw you, the fire made your tattoo glow as if it was liquid. It was my mind playing tricks as I thought you were Yama."

"Is that all that made you surmise that I was the Lord of Death?"

Surya looked down and slowly spoke, abashedly. "At the hotel, I looked up the internet to find more information on Yama and what surprised me was that he had been cursed with an infected leg. His stepmother or maid had cursed him."

Dharam laughed a little and said, "And you connected that story with my limp?"

Surya looked at him, embarrassed and said, "I know you explained that you had had an accident with a motorbike but everything was adding up to support my random thought so this added one more 'proof' to my theory."

Dharam said, "Since you are so interested in Yama, I will tell you his story. Let us first stop for a small cup of chai and then walk toward your hotel and sit on the steps. I know a perfect place for us to rest. You do have time, don't you?"

Surya nodded and Dharam continued, "I hope you are not feeling cold. And do not worry," he continued, smiling at his joke, "I will not charge you any fees as a guide for this."

Dharam led the way to a small tea stall and ordered two special chais.

"I did not know you get chai so late in a small place like Varanasi," said Surya.

"It's not that late," said Dharam, looking at his mobile phone, "It's just a little past 9 p.m. Varanasi has street food available through the night." As they waited for their little cups of heaven, Dharam started his narration, "People think of Yama as a tall, dark, ferocious man with a twirling mustache, wielding a mace. This imagery is from storybooks and comics, which depict him as the Lord of Death and so they project the horrors of death onto Yama.

Yama is actually the son of Surya, the Lord of the Sun," said Dharam smiling, "so in a way, he is your son."

"Ha-ha," laughed Surya, "with that analogy, you are my son, for you are Dharam Raj."

"Yes father," said Dharam and continued, "Surya, the Sun God, had a son called Manu, from whose name we get Manav or mankind. He is the first man on Earth and the father of all mankind."

"So, Manu is like Adam, in Hindu mythology."

"Yes, if you want to think so, but he is more like a mixture of Adam and Noah from the Biblical books.

Manu was told of a flood by a fish, who was none other than the *Matsya* avatar of Vishnuji. Manu built a boat and tied it to the horn that grew on the head of the fish. The fish kept getting larger and Manu and the Vedas were the sole survivors of the flood."

"It is so similar to the Noah story," said Surya, "I am sure that both must have originated during a global rise in water levels in a distant past."

"Possibly, but the similarity ends there. Manu is the generic name for the first man in every cycle of Creation. So, this Manu is the son of the Sun God and there have been other Manus in the past and will be more in the future."

"I am aware of the cycles of Creation," said Surya, "in fact, we were discussing it yesterday on the boat. But why are we discussing Manu?"

"Manu is the elder brother of Yama. Surya had twins after Manu, who he called Yama and Yami. People say Yami is the river Yamuna but that is just speculation. Yama was a nice young boy, a lad with a strong moral code, much like his elder brother, Manu.

But poor Yama – much cursed, oft-misunderstood and unfairly depicted. Yama was never a God to be feared, nor does he rule hell, in fact, he was not even a God; he was just an early mortal created to inhabit the Earth.

When his mother, Sanjana, was pregnant with twins, she went to her father's house for the delivery. Yama, the name itself, means twins in Sanskrit. Her husband, Surya, the Sun God, came to visit her. He smiled at seeing his pregnant wife; however, as she saw her husband's brilliance, she covered her eyes with her hands to shield herself from his light. Surya mistook her action as displeasure in seeing him and he uttered a curse; you will give birth to a son who everyone will fear and a daughter who will be weak. Thus, were born the twins Yama and his sister Yami, cursed within the womb.

While the elder brother Manu was the first man on Earth, Yama was the first man on Earth to die; he became a guide to other people who died later on; showing them the passage from life to death and thereafter. Slowly, he has been merged with the concept of death, being depicted as a giant, black in color, fearful. He was in reality, an intelligent and good-natured lad."

"How did he get a deformed leg?" asked Surya, now amused that he had mistaken the guide for the Lord of Death.

"Ah," said Dharam, "that is Yama's second curse. It is an interesting story; Sanjana came back to Surya's house with her newborn babies, Yama and Yami. She realized that the intensity that blazed from her husband was too strong for her. She found her skin tanning and gradually turning black, due to which the gods often called her Sandhya, which means evening or dusk. She decided to solve the situation and created a clone of herself, whom she called Chaya. Sanjana requested Chaya to impersonate her and take care of her husband and children for some time, while she took a break. Leaving Chaya to handle her household, Sanjana went for a period of rest to her father's house.

Surya, unknowing of the switch, treated Chaya as his wife and soon she gave birth to a son, Shani. Once she had children of her own, Chaya's treatment toward Yama and Yami became step-motherly. Yama was a precocious child and he found it strange that his mother should be unkind to him and his twin sister, so he set out and discovered the truth that Chaya was a replacement and not his real mother. One day, when Chaya scolded him, he kicked her calling her an imposter. The angry Chaya cursed the foot that kicked her; she cursed that it be deformed and eaten by maggots. When Surya returned home that evening and heard of the curse, he realized that no mother would curse her own child as Chaya had and discovered the truth of the switch. He gave a rooster to his son Yama, who ate out all the maggots from his leg, but the poor boy was yet left with a limp."

They finished sipping the tea and Dharam said, "Let me walk you to the hotel. There is a temple on the way that is perfect for you to visit with me."

"Why is that so?" asked Surya curiously.

"Because the temple is called the Yama Aditya temple. I, Dharam, am supposed to be Yama and you, Surya, are to be Aditya, the sun. So, this temple is for both of us, the Yama Aditya temple."

"That is really a coincidence," said Surya.

"Yes, it is," smiled Dharam, "What is even more special is that this temple is supposed to have been built by none other than Yama himself."

They walked slowly toward the hotel. The night was cold and black, a stray terracotta lamp floated by them in the inky river that silently flowed beside them.

"Yama is well known to all," said Surya, "but what about his twin sister?"

Dharam continued his story as they walked languorously. "Yami loved her brother, maybe a little too much and as she reached puberty, she suggested an incestuous relationship. The righteous Yama refused, saying it was sinful and against Dharma, but Yami persisted, wanting a child from her brother.

Yami persevered and said it would be sinful only if someone saw the sin being committed but the virtuous Yama said, 'The gods watch. Sex is not advisable within the family and neither should one copulate with the gods as onlookers.'

Yami insisted and claimed that the gods themselves had committed enough disgraceful actions in the past. Yama, the upright, retorted that they had never borne children from those actions. Besides, each generation should grow forward instead of committing the mistakes of their forefathers, he advised his sister.

Soon, Yama voluntarily chose death and became the first man to die, but Yami lived on, inconsolable at the loss of her twin. The twins loved each other. Legend has it that we celebrate the festival of *Bhau Beej,* during the festival of Diwali, on the second day of the moon to celebrate this sibling love between Yama and Yami. Men visit their sisters' house; she puts the red vermillion *tikka* on their forehead. The brothers carry gifts for their sisters and eat a meal cooked by her. This is because, on this day, Yama visits Yami, and a lamp is lit in honor of the Lord of Death who comes to visit Yami each year, no matter how busy he may be.

The father gave Yama the position of Lord of Dharma, Yami who earlier was worshiped as Mother Shakti became the fickle river Yamuna and Shani his stepbrother, a troubled, perplexed, oft-rejected child became Saturn the planet that affects Dharma. Even now, when Shani appears on the astrological charts, people get worried about the initial ill effects that he can bring until he starts to shine and prosper in the later periods of the lives of people he influences."

"Did Yama have any children?" asked Surya.

"Oh, yes, he did. He had one daughter whose son Vena was the opposite of his grandfather; a grandson who was extremely adharmic but is remembered because his murder led to the Creation of the Earth. Among the best-known children of Yama is Yudhishthira, the eldest Pandava. If you read the *Mahabharata*, then you must know that Mother Kunti's son, Yuddhisthira, the eldest Pandava, is the son of Dharamraj, the son of Yama himself."

"Why would Kunti call Yama to mate as her first choice?" wondered Surya aloud.

"It was Pandu, Kunti's husband who suggested that she beget a son from the Lord of Justice, the Dharamraj. It is only in later generations that Yama got the unfair depiction I told you about. He has been one of the original gods in the Hindu Pantheon, a keeper of Justice and Dharma, one of the most learned of the scriptures, wise and virtuous. Over time, people have merged him with *Mrityu*, who is Death, and given him all the characteristics of a fearful, demon-like predator."

They reached the steps to the temple and Dharam indicated they should sit there for a while.

Surya said, "You said Yama chose to die. How is that part of Dharma?"

Dharam said, "Our ancient texts provide for voluntary death, provided it is announced in advance to the community. It must be a formal declaration. If you have a terminal illness, or you can see death approaching and your physical condition is so bad that life is of no meaning."

"I am surprised euthanasia is condoned in the ancient texts," said Surya

"It is more than euthanasia, for even a householder is allowed to voluntarily die if he has completed his responsibilities and has no desire to live further."

Surprised Surya asked, "And how are you supposed to give up your life voluntarily?"

Dharam said softly, "There are many ways mentioned and each has its own merit and methodology. But the most acceptable ways specified are abstaining from eating or fasting to death as done by the good King Parikshit but there are others like death by water and death by fire. Kunti and Gandhari who lived in the forest as a hermit after the *Mahabharata* war chose this method and did not flee the approaching flames of a forest fire. The Pandava brothers too killed themselves by yet another method mentioned by the scriptures, you keep walking northwards until you can."

"Oh my God," exclaimed Surya, "this has been an eye-opener. But it is Yama who surprises me; he was just a mortal, the first to die and we have elevated him to the status of the Lord of Death."

Dharam smiled, and once again Surya seemed transfixed in the smile. The air around seemed to thicken like a blanket being cast upon them. "They don't exist," he said softly.

Surya looked at him puzzled and Dharam closed his eyes. "Yama and all the others are not gods," he said. "It is we who make mortals into gods. In all religions, there is mythology and there are prophets who lived years ago; yet today, we fight wars in their names, prejudice ourselves in our belief. We believe in gods who maim the nose of women, and their offspring who walk on water and their prophets who marry prepubescent girls. We raise swords and kill in their names but the fact is that none truly existed. We need to look inwards rather than outwards, to grow spiritually and develop instead of staying rooted in old stories that have been told to us. We need to use the mythological tales to help us think and ponder, to take an essence of what is being said but not to literally follow each word as if it were written by God or uttered by an archangel.

For many of the narrators themselves were mortals like you and me, some have crossed the line ahead, the same line that we are all looking to reach and cross ourselves."

"So, after all the stories of Yama that I have heard these past few days, you are telling me he does not exist?

We are in the city that deals in death, where Yama is everywhere and I have to come to Varanasi to know he is a myth?"

"Yes," said Dharam, "You need to come here to know that death itself does not exist, death is a myth. You are right, this is the city about death but the reigning Lord of the city is not Yama, it is Shiva. Yama is none other than Siva, who holds within him the duality of the twins, Yama and Yami, life and death, female and male, dharma and adharma, vairagya and householder."

They sat for a few moments, and Dharam rose. "The temple is just up a few steps, let us go there."

"Will it be open at this hour?" asked Surya.

"It usually shuts by ten o'clock at night but I know the priest well. It is a really small temple."

The cloak of winter seemed to grow closer around them and Surya felt a chill. Involuntarily, the hair on his hand stood up trying to retain the heat of his body, and his teeth let out a small chatter.

"You are cold, sir," said Dharam, "I am sorry I have kept you out so late. Let us rush to the warmth of the temple, maybe the priest will lend us a shawl or mix us a warm drink."

They climbed the few steps and entered the little temple built by the God of Death. The temple was not shut and the priest was nowhere to be seen. As they entered the temple, Surya was mesmerized as he saw the twin idols; he felt a plethora of emotions overcome him and he sat on the floor. No longer was he shivering cold, his mind was full of thoughts as he recognized the Shivling from his dreams, the familiar black stone idol that had been beckoning him in his sleep; at last, he had found it. Strange questions arose in his mind, as he stared at the little Shivling; questions that he had never voiced before even to himself. *Why did you call me here? What do you want me to do now that I have found you? Why did my baby have to die before even being born? You do know that I have nothing really to live for. Why am I even living? Is there a purpose to my existence? Should I be a vairagya or a householder?* Somewhere in the background, he could hear Dharam's voice saying, "You see my point, sir, in the Yama temple too, there is a Shivling. There is no Yama, there is no death, just one continuum of waves, up and down, on and off." His voice blurred as tears began slipping out of Surya's eye and he reached out to touch the statue that had called him. *What is my mission here, why did you call me?* and he clasped the little idol that stood in front of him. Somewhere far away he heard a bull grunting and then everything dissolved for him as he slipped into the void, into the nothing, into a bliss of no color, no space or time, melting into the Shivling. In that bliss, he knew all the answers, he knew there were no questions, he understood everything and nothing at the same time, dualities as he felt himself within the lingam.

CHAPTER 8

VARANASI, DAY THREE, MORNING

*"When your soul is perfectly seated in your body,
the dance begins automatically, and when you
dance you do not dance alone."*

—*Shiva Purana*

Amrit woke up with a start; for a minute he was confused as to where he was and then remembered he was in Varanasi. He picked up his phone from the bedside table to check the time; it was four o'clock in the morning. It will be perfect to sit in front of the hotel, on the steps of the river Ganga and meditate. He had been doing pre-sunrise meditation using a diya at home; *what better opportunity than to do it here?* he thought to himself. Slowly, for he was in no hurry, he rose and stretched himself. In about twenty minutes, he was downstairs at the lobby to ask for a candle or hurricane lamp; he was surprised to see that there was activity at the reception desk at such an early hour. "Varanasi wakes up before dawn," the receptionist said. "There is the morning Ganges boat ride that takes place at 5 a.m.," he continued, as he hunted for the candle and matches, "we have to provide for the wake-up calls and bed tea."

Amrit went outside the hotel toward the ghats. It was dark, but as his eyes got familiar with the darkness, he could see other figures sitting along the riverside at a distance. Temple bells were ringing far away for the morning aarthi and he could see tiny flames of diyas as people started the first prayer of the day. Amrit seated himself on a little mattress that the hotel had provided for its guests and pulled the shawl around him a little tighter for it was chilly at that early hour. He decided to first do his breathing exercises before he lit the candle for meditation. It was exhilarating to be doing pranayamas on the banks of the Ganga. He took in more than just the air and its primordial scents: he took in all of the ancient city of Kashi as he inhaled and he would expel his bad energy in controlled exhalation. As the dark skies turned deep gray, maybe about thirty minutes before the sun rose in the eastern sky, he decided to start concentrating on the candle flame. As he lit the wick, he heard footsteps approaching and he turned around to see who it was. In the darkness, he could see a silhouette limping toward the hotel.

"Namaste Amritji," the person said. Amrit peered to figure out who the stranger was, although he automatically replied, "Namaste." The person approached closer and Amrit saw that it was Dharam, their guide. "I am sorry I didn't recognize you initially, in this darkness," said Amrit apologetically, "but why are you here so early?"

"I have come to take a guest of the hotel for the sunrise cruise this morning."

"So early?" said Amrit, "I thought the boats leave at five in the morning?"

"I have reached a bit earlier than needed," said Dharam. "But you are awake early too," he continued, "I did not realize that you are such a serious student of yoga. I am sorry I have disturbed you."

"Oh no, don't worry, it is no disturbance. I started my yoga exercises a few years ago," said Amrit smiling, "My day does not seem complete without it, now. Sitting here in the cool dawn, in front of the majestic river, it is even more fulfilling. Do you do yoga as well?"

"In Varanasi, we are brought up with yoga around us. Of course, Rishikesh is the center of yoga, but here in Varanasi too, it is taught everywhere, in our schools, at home. My father was a teacher of yoga and I am well versed in the practices. I saw you lighting the candle for tratak meditation. Do you also use body locks when doing it?"

"Body locks?" asked Amrit, his voice full of puzzlement, "I have never heard of it."

"There are three *bandhs* or locks. If you practice them while doing certain asanas, then it can help you increase the chakra energy."

Amrit felt a wave of excitement rise within himself. "I have wanted to awaken the Kundalini, but they say you must do it under supervision only."

"I can certainly show you the practice. Since you are already aware of the chakras and you meditate on them, you can increment it with breathing with body locks to jumpstart the process. If you want, I can show it to you in your room."

"Do you have the time?" Amrit asked. "I do not want any guest to be delayed on my account."

"Do not worry. As I said, I have reached early. I will explain it to you and then you can practice it on your own."

The two of them proceeded to the room and Amrit spread a mat on the floor. He sat in the lotus position and Dharam asked him to normalize his breath in both nostrils through pranayama counts. He then explained how to lock the muscles at the anus by clamping them up tight. "That activates the basal chakra of the Earth element, the one with the red lotus," he said gently. He then moved upwards explaining the second lock by pulling the stomach muscles inwards toward the back to form an abdominal lock. Amrit tried it, his tiny stomach pulled in tight. "This will activate the solar plexus chakra of the fire element," said Dharam, "the lotus with the yellow petals." Finally, he explained to bend the head down at the neck, the chin toward the chest, forming a third lock at the throat. "This will activate the thyroid gland, the chakra of space and ether," he said.

"Practice the *beej* mantras of the chakras using these three locks at different times and sometimes together," said Dharam, "and the coiled snake will rise if you are ready."

"I have been doing chakra meditation for the past few months," said Amrit excitedly, "I will now try it with these added locks."

With that, Dharam took his leave and Amrit started the chanting of the beej mantra for each chakra, working from the base of the spine, upwards, in seven energy spots, concentrating on the colors and lotus petals and adding the three new locks that he had just learned. By the time, he had reached the point at the top of the head, the multi-petal lotus with the Shivling at the center, he felt at peace and serene. A white light flashed inside him; the brightness so strong that it blinded him even as his eyes were closed. An electric current ran up his spine, the white light turned metallic like the gleaming of stainless steel and it took on the different hues as it moved upward along his back. He writhed out of the lotus position as the electric charge within him increased in intensity as it rose; he lay in a heap, convulsing, his mouth opened, his eyes semi-closed in a trance, as Shakti climbed from his base, slithering slowly over each vertebra until it reached the neck and then crawling into the skull to meet her paramour, Shiva, at the top of his head. He was in utter bliss and yet a never-ending electric current passed through him; he lay in a fetus like position, in communion with the Universe. In what seemed like a few minutes, but in reality, was a few hours, he saw a blueness spread in his inner mind; a color so deep, so rich and so blue that he knew he would not see anything else in his life that was bluer than this shade. His mind flashed with images of different symbols, sometimes a lotus, other times a bull but always getting back to the still deep blue that was haunting him and drawing him to it. He jumped into the blueness, although the color was within him and saw a single ripple in the clean surface as his body leaped inside. He realized that he had jumped into the navel of a blue God, into the *nabhi*, the belly button of blueness. All was calm, all ripples ironed out as he lay within the body of Shiva, and with that thought, he passed out.

Amrit woke and shook himself. He looked at his phone and realized that three hours had elapsed. There was a missed call from Gagan and several messages from him and others but he had been oblivious to it all. He knew that his visit to Varanasi had been fruitful; he had been called here for this experience, he put his palms together and chanted '*Om Namah Shivaya*' a few times and bowed down to the energy that permeated through every molecule around him and silently thanked the voice that had whispered "Varanasi" in his head when he had cremated his mother.

AFTERWORD

I have used the mystical city of Kashi as the location of the story because I love it but it could be any place, for it rests within us. Varanasi or any mythical city is the place we go to in our minds, to find the answers we seek. It is where we will find a resolution to the day-to-day issues like understanding the dualities around us as well as fundamental questions that exist in our mind and soul, a communion with the energy that lies within each of us.

While the book speaks of three distinct characters, they all merge to different aspects of one person, living within us. Sometimes it is one aspect exerting more control while others stay in the shadows: whether it is Surya who acts on his dreams, desperately searching happiness, unsure whether to be a householder or a wanderer or Amrit who hears the voices of unreconciled pasts, who learns to accept the sexuality that lies overt or latent in all people, Rajat who speaks within us to find reason, patterns and logical explanations, and prevents us from letting go. Dharam, Prabod, Rajbir, Mrinalini, Nayana, Damyanti dwell in us, in different measures and speak up at different times of our lives.

GLOSSARY

Aai — Mother (in Marathi, an Indian language)

Amreeka — America as pronounced by many local South Asian people

Asanas — Body positions in yoga

Atma — The personal self (consciousness)

Aum, Om — Sacred sound (Indian religions)

Baba — Father (in Marathi, an Indian language)

Balaji — Vishnu

Beej — Seed

Benaras — Another name for Varanasi

Bhrighu — One (of seven) great (and immortal) sages

Chaat — Street food of savory snacks

Chakras — Wheels of energy

Chatai — Straw mat

Darshan — Literally sight, means getting to see an image or holy person

Deva — A divine being, masculine

Dharma — Universal laws governing all people

Diya — Earthen lamp

Ganga Jal	– Water from the river Ganges, believed to be holy water
Ghat	– A flight of steps, on the banks leading into rivers
Ghee	– Clarified butter
Gulley	– A narrow alley
Jhalmuri	– A popular snack from Bengal, spicy, made of puffed rice
Kachori	– An Indian savory snack
Kashi	– An older name for Varanasi
Khichdi	– An Indian dish of cereal (usually rice) and lentils
Kulhad	– Traditional clay cup without a handle
Mahadev	– Shiv
Malai toast	– Cream and sugar on top of buttered toast
Mandir	– Temple
Matsya avatar	– An avatar of Vishnu, one of the ten, where he appears as a fish
Mirchi and masala	– Literally a mixture of spices but used to denote things that create excitement and interest
Moksh	– Liberation, enlightenment, release
Nabhi	– Navel, belly button
Paan	– Betel leaves filled with nuts and assorted edibles which South Asian's chew

Pranayama — Breath control and breathing exercises in yoga

Ram naam satya hai — Everything will die but only the name of God (ram) will stay forever

Roti — Indian bread

Saab — Mister, respectfully

Saree — An Indian traditional garment worn by women, consisting of a long single piece of cloth

Sudarshan Chakra — Spinning, disk-shaped weapon, associated with Vishnu, with 108 serrated edges

Tandav — Divine dance (associated with Shiva) and in one form, could lead to destruction

Tikka — A small mark of (usually vermillion) powder out on the forehead, usually symbolic

Tikki — A small cake

Tratak — Form of meditation, involving staring at a candle or an external or internal point, combined with breath control

Yagna — A ritualistic offering or sacrifice for a specific purpose

Yamraj — Yama, God of Death

Yuga — One (out of four) of the ages of the world

Made in the USA
Columbia, SC
26 December 2020